Rac

Samantha Alexander lives in Lincolnshire with her son, husband and a variety of animals including her thoroughbred horse, Bunny, and a pet goose called Bertie. Her schedule is almost as busy and exciting as her plots – she writes a number of columns for newspapers and magazines, is an agony aunt for teenagers on BBC Radio Leeds and in her spare time she regularly competes in dressage and showjumping events.

WINNERS 1
Racing Start

Samantha Alexander

MACMILLAN CHILDREN'S BOOKS

To my dearest husband.
For your endless love, support and encouragement.

First published 2001 by Macmillan Children's Books
a division of Pan Macmillan Limited
20 New Wharf Road, London N1 9RR
Basingstoke and Oxford
www.panmacmillan.com

Associated companies throughout the world

ISBN 0 330 48438 9

3 5 7 9 8 6 4 2

A CIP catalogue record for this book is available from
the British Library.

Phototypeset by Intype London Ltd
Printed and bound in Great Britain by Mackays of Chatham plc, Kent

One

The rain poured down – great driving sheets of it – sending the racehorses crazy.

"You can't!" Shona was horrified at what I'd suggested. Her mouth dropped open with the shock of it. But then Tralligan, the horse she was riding, fly-bucked towards the rails and, fighting to calm him, she couldn't say any more.

I glanced fearfully towards the horsebox where Jacko, the travelling head lad, was ringing the Guv'nor on his mobile phone. He hadn't heard me. He was hunched into his sheepskin coat just wanting to go home.

I tightened the reins on Sergeant Peggy, resolve strengthening with every second.

None of them understood. The fire, the drive, the passion, the need. They thought I was a dreamer. They thought I'd probably give up, broken-hearted, and go into nursing or teaching. They didn't believe that I would be the youngest jockey and the first female to win the Grand National.

The cab door clunked open, startling the horses. Jacko jumped down, smiling for the first time that day. "That's it, chop, chop. Back in the box. The Guv'nor's called it off." He was all ready with head collars and horse boots.

It was the end of race day. The two horses were meant to be schooled round the course now everybody had gone home, but the professional jockey hadn't shown and the going had turned from soft to treacherous. Shona jumped off gratefully, pulling at the girth straps and sidestepping a cow kick.

Not me though. For me, every muscle and sinew was locked with tension. This was it – the moment.

Shona glanced across, panic starting to show in her face but then fading to "please yourself, I don't care".

Sergeant Peggy always took advantage of indecision. Arching her back, she sprang up on her hind legs. I clung to her neck, snatching at the silky fine mane that ran through my fingers. I clamped my knees to the tiny race saddle, the spell broken, blood pumping into every limb.

"What the?" Jacko moved forward, hand outstretched.

But my mind was crystal clear. As soon as Sergeant Peggy came down on all fours, I ripped off the quarter sheet tucked under my knees and threw it at Jacko.

The mare leapt forward, snagging at the bit. That's when I gave her her head and touched the hard chestnut flanks with my stick.

"The Guv'nor'll kill yer," Jacko's voice carried in the gale.

But it was too late. I'd turned towards the grandstand and the toughest jump on the course. Sergeant Peggy rocketed forward, ears pricked, eyeing up the stiff birch.

I had no choice. This was my only chance to prove myself. Nobody took girls seriously, not in racing. It was a man's world. But I was going to change that. From the age of five I'd dreamt of this. I used to rig up a saddle on the back of the sofa – the handle of an egg whisk as one stirrup and a potato masher for the other. I used to ride race finishes while everybody else watched television. I could read form before I could tie shoelaces and I knew fifty different facts about Red Rum.

Now I was hijacking the best racehorse at Dolphin Barn and trying to impress Kenneth Brown, a governor with a fearsome reputation.

Sergeant Peggy quickened her stride, slapping through the gluey ground. I was right, she would operate on the heavy ground – she just needed a jump ahead of her ... A sheet of rain fogged my

vision for a split second. And then it was on us –
five foot, solid, ungiving and uphill.

I leant back, the breath locking in my throat.
Generations of jockeys had called this the "bowel
mover". Now I knew why.

I had to see a good stride. A perfect stride. This
was the secret of being a top jump jockey – I
hadn't studied videos of John Francome for
nothing. Sergeant Peggy tensed, holding back,
suddenly worried.

"Come on, my lovely." I stroked her soaked
neck, praying she wouldn't bottle out.

We were close to the rails, picking out the best
ground, travelling well. Now I had to ask her to
lengthen her stride. It was all down to the next
few seconds . . . Please let the Guv'nor be
watching.

I didn't see the figure running towards us. I
concentrated purely on staying with the movement, leaning in close, keeping my hands still. A
rush of adrenalin burst through my veins as the
mare took off and soared upwards. We'd got it
right. Perfection.

She corkscrewed left. My neck cricked back
and I crumpled forward. She fell hard on her
nose, skidding a few metres with her legs trapped
under her. I shot forward, thrown clear, the breath
rushing out of my lungs.

The angry voice sounded far away, but then I
could see somebody catching the mare, running

expert hands down her legs. I turned over, bruised and sick with dread. I couldn't breathe and my mouth was full of dirt.

Rory Calligan blurred in and out of focus. Rory, up and coming National Hunt jockey, eighteen, with half the female population chasing him. I recognized him from the picture blu-tacked inside my school locker. I thought of Rory every night, after I'd thought of Becher's Brook and before I went to sleep.

"If you've got an explanation I can't think what it is." His brown eyes, usually soft and crinkled, narrowed into steely slits. He seemed oblivious of the biting rain and the blood pumping out of my nose. But Sergeant Peggy was all right. That was all I cared about.

I tried to stand up but wobbled. If he wasn't such a pig he'd scoop me into his arms like they do in period dramas. This wasn't how I'd pictured our first meeting.

"What's your name?"

Who did he think he was? "Justina Brooks." I tried not to show my teeth which were probably stained bright red.

"Next time you want a holiday job, Justina, try hairdressing." I could see his Adam's apple straining to swallow a smirk.

I wasn't going to tell him that I'd tried that already but that I'd been fired for missing work to go the Grand National.

He held out a helping hand – at long last. "Rory Calligan," he said quite normally.

I wasn't going to pass up the chance of body contact even if he was a pig. His oilskin blew open showing the grey and blue silks from the last race. I knew, despite everything, it would be a week before I washed the hand that he'd held.

"If you're OK, the Guv'nor wants to see you. He saw everything from the Grandstand."

I felt as if ice cubes had been poured down my back.

He turned to lead Sergeant Peggy back to the horsebox, any interest in me gone.

"You know that last race?" I said peevishly. "You rode it all wrong. Tony McCoy wouldn't have got boxed in."

"I have never, in all my years as a racehorse trainer, seen such a display of insolence." The Guv'nor paced up and down in the tiny cluttered office, ashen with anger.

I shrank back into the hard chair, wishing I could hide behind the huge oil painting of a racehorse called Dolphin.

The Guv'nor was a fearsome character. He had wild haunted eyes which never missed a trick. He lived, ate, slept, breathed racehorses and expected everyone else to do the same. He was ridiculously superstitious. He'd worn the same clothes to races for twenty years, thinking they were lucky. He avoided the colour green like the plague and never seemed to brush his hair properly. He went everywhere with a wire haired terrier called Chelsea who was equally aggressive. He was not to be messed with, especially not by a fifteen year old girl convinced she was going to be a champion jockey.

"So, what have you got to say for yourself?" he barked.

I shrugged, taken aback, expecting him to rant on for at least another ten minutes. The lattice of broken veins on his cheeks throbbed purple. Chelsea growled from under the table where she was guarding five hundred packets of Polo mints meant for the horses.

"I'm sorry," I mumbled, dripping water on to the carpet, completely sodden from head to toe.

"Have you any idea how much hassle I've had taking you on?"

Kenneth Brown was the only trainer in Cheltenham who had given me a chance, and that was after nearly pestering him to death. I knew it had annoyed the other staff who'd been to racing college first.

I stared at the bay racehorse in the picture. Kenny Brown had trained horses for twenty years. Dolphin was his only Grand National winner. He was nearly as hungry for another win as I was.

"The mare fell because she was startled, but you should have been ready. You can't switch off and admire the scenery just because you've put a horse right at a fence."

This is what I usually loved, the analysis, the what ifs, the maybes, the if onlys. The whole buzz of racing talk. It gave me a funny warm feeling inside. But not today. Today I was too scared of what the Guv'nor was about to say.

"I want you to go home and do your GCSEs. I don't want to see you or hear your name mentioned."

Panicky tears sprang to my eyes. He couldn't be serious. I'd worked my brains out for him. "You can't be . . ." Words died in my throat. He really meant it. His eyes were like granite.

"Then, if you still want a life of unsocial hours, primitive housing, no privacy, and lousy pay, I'd like you to come back as an apprentice."

"He got rid of you, then?" Shona's eyes lit up expectantly.

Scooby, one of the other lads and always easy to pick out because he wore a red woolly hat with a pom pom over his jockey skull cap, was coming out of a stable carrying a muck bag. He was oozing sympathy. "Never mind, luv, he might change his mind."

I couldn't tell anyone. I kept my new knowledge close to me like something precious.

Instead, I ran down the first row of twenty stables kissing each racehorse on the nose, apart from Tralligan who was liable to bite it off. Badger, the head lad, was clattering along with the feed trolley, complaining I was crackers. I wrapped my arms tight round my sides and spun round, faint specks of rain catching in my hair.

"Goodbye, Dolphin Barn," I whispered. "I'll be back. Just you wait and see. And next time as a jockey . . ."

Two

"A National Hunt jockey can expect to fall every tenth race." Mum crashed into first gear and then shot forwards at a crossroads. "It's statistics – I heard it on Channel Four's Race Line."

I closed my eyes, willing her to shut up. For the last two months, Mum had made it her business to research every gruesome detail about racing. It hadn't put me off.

"We never expected this, Justina. I don't mind you having a year out to get this jockey thing out of your system if that's what it takes, but let me book an appointment at St Martin's, it's the best place for A-levels, they're always in the top hundred."

I still hadn't opened my eyes. I focused on the sun warming my face and the tingle of excitement in my stomach as Dolphin Barn drew closer.

"Justina?"

The problem with having parents who are lawyers is that they expect you to follow in their footsteps. Mum could have been a barrister before she gave it up to have a family, so when I passed nine GCSEs with seven A grades she took it for granted that I'd be following family tradition. She was asking the impossible. I couldn't give up horses. I needed them like I needed air.

We swept up the long drive towards the stables, railed paddocks on each side. I craned to see some of the horses while Mum patted her hair, looking at her reflection in the interior mirror. It was August, the start of the winter jump season wasn't too far off. Soon the seventy stables would be buzzing with life and vitality.

The knot in my stomach tightened. There he was, the Guv'nor, examining a horse led out by Scooby. It was Leonora, a sorrel mare with two white socks who, I'd later discover, would be in my care.

"Ah, Joanna." The Guv'nor touched his threadbare flat cap. "Mrs Bird."

"Brooks," Mum corrected, tight-lipped. "And it's Justina."

The Guv'nor always got everybody's name wrong, even that of Badger, the head lad who'd been at Dolphin for over twenty years. Mum was offended. I could tell by the way she was picking bits off her clothes. I prayed she wouldn't say anything, and it must have been telepathic because Scooby hastily passed Leonora to another lad and picked up my suitcase. "Right then, the cottage it is."

Each lad looked after two horses at Dolphin and lived in the hostel which had been built on to the main yard. He had his meals there, slept in bunk beds and had a communal room with a pool table and dart board. The girls, Mandy and Shona, lived in a tumbledown cottage which had dry rot and dodgy plumbing.

Scooby pushed open the back door and thumped my suitcase down on the lino. Mum bristled at the sight of a pile of dirty pots in the sink and a string of bras drying on top of the radiator. A mountain of jodphurs buried the fridge, which probably had more fur inside it than the tabby kitten helping itself to a chocolate cake on the table.

Mum took one look and marched straight back to the car. "Let me know when you've had enough," she clipped. "I'll pick you up at the end of the drive." After an icy peck on the cheek she drove off, disappointed and probably despairing. But I'd got what I wanted. An apprenticeship at one of the best yards in Cheltenham. I was going to ride races – and win.

"Brooks, get up here quick – second lot's out in ten minutes."

Tralligan was one of the best horses in the yard and much sought after with the lads. If their horse won a race they always got extra money. The Guv'nor had taken Tralligan away from Jacko and given him to me.

"You'll be popular now." Mandy, pink-faced and always out of breath, jogged upsides.

"Circle wide, keep on the move," Badger shouted. The Guv'nor drove on up the gallops where he'd watch through binoculars. A whole aviary had come alive in my stomach. My knees were shaking as I stood up in the micro-short stirrups. Everybody was watching, but Jacko watched most closely, black eyes narrowed. He looked like a little boy who'd had his sweets snatched away. But he'd obviously done something to upset the Guv'nor. That was the only reason I'd got his horse.

"Hey, Scooby," Jacko shouted, breaking into a trot, "what do you call a girl who thinks she's going to be the first chick to win the Grand National?"

Scooby shrugged. He slouched in the saddle, clearly not wanting to take sides.

"Bumper Velvet!" Jacko shouted triumphantly so everybody within a hundred kilometre radius could hear. Bumpers were the lowest form of jump races.

My cheeks prickled hot.

"Ignore him," Mandy whispered.

"Less of the wisecracks, Jacko." Badger watched the horses circle with an eagle eye. "OK,

13

Justina and Harris, upsides. Three quarter gallop. No flash stunts."

I swallowed hard and steered Tralligan away from the group. I'd never done work ride before. This is what the horses did every day on the flat to reach full fitness. They always worked in pairs and a good work rider concentrated on settling the horse and not allowing the gallop to develop into a race.

Harris lined up, leathery-faced and unfriendly. I knew every pair of eyes was turned my way. Most of them wanted me to fail – but I wasn't going to give them the satisfaction.

Tralligan leapt forward, finding the bit. I arched over his neck, pushing my weight down into the feather-light stirrups. The wind sucked the breath out of my mouth. My eyes streamed. White rails flashed by. Tralligan thundered up the hill, itching to get past the other horse. I sat up a little, focused on rhythm, keeping the big horse together. He slowed back, settled, dropped his head into his work.

It was over too quickly. We pulled up and turned the horses to walk back on a loose rein. Already the next pair were pounding up the ancient turf, stride for stride.

It was exhilarating. "That was fantastic." I patted Tralligan over and over, ruffling his mane. Harris didn't say a word, he looked as if he'd just

14

put the kettle on instead of having galloped up a hillside on a racehorse.

"How did I do?" The words gushed out. The Guv'nor stood po-faced, examining his binoculars. Chelsea sat at his feet, pulling equally grim faces and showing yellow teeth.

"I'll tell you when you've made a mistake. Otherwise you'll do your work and say nowt." I presume what he really meant was I'd done OK.

The horses jogged home, steaming. I kept at the back of the string as nobody would talk to me anyway. It was so different from last season when nobody minded me tidying the muck heap and cleaning the Guv'nor's car. But then as a dogsbody I wasn't a threat, not like I was as an apprentice.

Shona rode upsides Jacko, leaning in close and whispering under her breath. I'd always had the knack of being able to tune into people's conversations. It isn't difficult once you've learnt to block out other noises. I soon discovered why he'd lost Tralligan. Jacko had been caught feeding information on runners to another yard – a sackable offence. And I learnt something else. The Guv'nor had kept him on because he rated him as a future jockey. A coldness settled over me as I realized I had serious competition . . .

Tralligan and Leonora made up for everything, although Tralligan was a seasoned campaigner who didn't like fuss. Leonora was a nervous, highly-strung filly who was finding a big race yard daunting. I spent hours grooming and befriending her, trying to get her to grow in confidence. While the others played football between two and four o'clock, I sat in her stable and talked to her.

That day I was the butt of endless practical jokes. At lunchtime I sat with a learner plate on my back without knowing. Somebody superglued my riding boots to the tack room floor. At evening stables I had the lowly job of scrubbing out the mash barrow, only somebody had poured in a whole tin of treacle to make it worse. When I finally got in for tea there was no food left. Good old Scooby, anticipating this trick, had put aside a plate of chips. They were stone cold and tasted of washing-up liquid but I didn't complain.

Everybody crowded into the hostel at seven-thirty to watch a repeat of Richard Dunwoody on *This is Your Life*. There were lots of oohs and aahs when Desert Orchid came on last and a few wolf whistles for his lass. Surprisingly they'd left a spare chair out for me. On closer examination I found it was occupied by a selection of brightly coloured maggots.

"They giving you a hard time?" Badger was doing his round as I headed back to the cottage later. He was dedicated to the horses and kept himself to himself.

I nodded dumbly.

"A little bird tells me yer want to win the National?"

Since second lot, the second work ride of the morning, the whole of the racing world seemed to know. I didn't deny it.

"Do yer not think that's a mite ambitious?"

"A girl's bound to win it one day. Why not me?"

I think he heard the irritation in my voice. He sucked in his cheeks. A notion suddenly hit me.

"Were you here when Dolphin . . ."

"Aye. And a finer horse you'd never find. When he took Becher's second time round we thought he was never going to touch the ground. The Guv'nor and me, we had tears running down our cheeks."

I was mesmerized. I couldn't hear enough.

"Anyway," he said as he snapped out of the past, "you'll not find an Aintree horse in this yard." The light went out of his eyes.

"Why?" I pushed, disappointed.

"It takes character. Not just ability. You need a horse that can practically talk. A National horse only comes along once in a lifetime and the Guv'nor's had his."

That night I snuggled gratefully under clean sheets, dreaming of Dolphin and how I'd have ridden him in the most difficult steeplechase of all time. Ridden him and won.

Three

In the beginning I made endless mistakes and Badger barked at me like a bulldog. If it wasn't him, it was the Guv'nor. Thoroughbreds were a different game to ponies and you always had to be one step ahead of them. They had to be rugged up to the eyeballs and watched over like the Bank of England. Woe betide anyone who hadn't noticed a cough or a filled leg. The horses were the most important things at Dolphin Barn. I fell into bed every night exhausted from early starts and long days, but not before I'd done squatting exercises to build up the racing muscles in my legs.

Mandy and Shona were disappointed that I wasn't one of them. Their sole ambition was marriage to a rich and famous jockey and they couldn't understand my obsession with becoming a race rider. They lived for gatecrashing race parties and for celebrity-spotting. I let them talk me into going to a jockey's ball one night and we slipped in free of charge under the marquee. I spent all night refusing to drink and got chatted up by a jockey old enough to be my father. After that I stayed at home every night with Smokey, the kitten, who curled up on my knee, or pounced on the television.

Things were tougher than I'd expected. I didn't have any real friends and I was aching with homesickness and disappointed with my apprenticeship. I hadn't been near a racecourse and there was no talk of a jockey's licence.

I was beginning to think that Mandy and Shona were right and I was chasing a pipe dream.

Things were getting more and more difficult. It was twenty-nine days since Dolphin Barn had had a winner and morale was low. Nobody cracked jokes. There were no more pranks. The Guv'nor stopped going to meets and watched television instead. Vets filed in and out taking blood tests and chuntering about viruses, but nothing was conclusive. Tralligan raced twice but tailed off. Something was definitely wrong.

In early October, racing stopped because of a freak cold spell. There was heavy frost. We were confined to the horse-walker and to riding in an indoor school. There were too many empty hours in the day and everyone was beginning to get on everyone else's nerves. Even the lads' football matches had been put on hold.

After second lot I usually cleaned tack in the huge tack room, filled with bridles and saddles and endless trunks of rugs. The racing saddles were the size of postage stamps and so light you had to hold them steady while you worked.

Shona usually did Jacko's tack while Mandy did Steve's. Steve had spiky, short, dyed blond hair and was very good-looking. I didn't have a crush on anybody there and only did my own.

One evening Jacko was sitting hogging the electric fire, eating a box of Mandy's chocolates and reading one of the tabloids. He read out loud, smug and condescending. " 'Old Faithful Brown Losing His Touch. Dolphin Barn couldn't even send out a Donkey Derby winner on present form. One has to ask the question, should trainers stand down after a certain age?' There you go." Jacko propped one boot on top of the other. "The old crock's passed it. Should do us all a favour and hang up his binoculars."

In a fury I grabbed the first thing that came to hand, a wring-out mop, and squeezed it all over Jacko's head.

"You cow!" He leapt up, spraying water everywhere. "You're crazy, do you know that?"

"That'll teach you to call the Guv'nor names," I rasped, throat tight with temper.

"That's enough." The Guv'nor was at the door.

"Oh no!" Shona stubbed out a cigarette, chalky with shock. Smoking was strictly against the rules.

The Guv'nor silenced everyone in a quarter of a second. "Racing's back on for Saturday. You'd better tell the others. I want those horses gleaming. If you don't come back with the best turned out horses this yard's ever seen, there'll be no football for a month."

"Did he hear?" Mandy had two bright pink spots on her cheeks.

"Well, if he didn't, he needs a hearing aid." Shona scooped up the tab end of her cigarette, which she'd kicked under the saddle horse.

"Aw, shoot," Jacko suddenly leapt backwards, shaking his trouser leg in a frenzy. Chelsea beetled out, jaws clamped round a chocolate. "That flaming dog," Jacko grimaced, "just peed on my leg."

That Saturday, racing was at Newbury and Sandown Park and we had horses at both. Both courses needed good jumpers with real stamina. The atmosphere in the yard was nail-bitingly tense. If we didn't have a winner, the Guv'nor would probably pack up racing and start breeding wire haired terriers. Twice, journalists rang sniffing for a story. Scooby told them his crystal ball had been smashed in a removals van. Luckily the Guv'nor didn't hear. He'd locked himself in the house with the television and *The Racing Post*.

Badger couldn't bear the tension as everyone crowded into the hostel to watch the first race, a

21

novice hurdle over two miles. Neither could I, so we decided to go to Cheltenham to pick up some saddlery repairs.

On the way we passed Cheltenham racecourse, the Mecca of racing and home of the Gold Cup. For six years running I'd stayed there for summer Pony Club camp and dreamt of being a jockey. We'd slept in the bunk beds meant for the stable lads and I once dreamt that I'd led Desert Orchid into the winner's enclosure and been kissed by Richard Dunwoody.

"Ruddy hell!" Badger slammed on the brakes and swerved on to the grass verge. I cricked my neck as I snapped out of my thoughts and the seat belt bit into my chest.

Five racehorses skittered and slid on the tarmac ahead of us. The lane was narrow and, because of a blind bend, we hadn't seen them coming. Badger screeched to a halt, accidentally catching the horn as he leapt out of the car, furious that highly strung horses had been taken out on such a dangerous road.

As I was scrabbling with my seat belt, a massive chestnut horse in the group suddenly panicked and leapt sideways over a thorn hedge. It happened in slow motion. The horse sprang from nothing and launched into the air, throwing its lad backwards and out of the saddle. The scrunch and thrash as it tore through the top of the hedge took me back two years, to when I'd pressed to the front of the crowd, pushing and shoving to see a sea of horses surge over Becher's. We waited for the chestnut to appear on the other side, fully expecting it to bomb off up the ploughed field. But there was nothing. Just a heavy thump. My memory flashed back to that day at Aintree – a picture of three horses straddling the monstrous ditch exploded in my head.

"It's in a ditch!" I yelled, tearing into action. I could hear it paddling, twisting, trying to get up. Badger was ahead of me, running through a gap in the hedge, slithering down the steep bank.

The horse was wedged at an angle on its side. It was stuck in a huge dyke, frightened and panicking, its neck and head sloshing in a foot of water.

"Keep its nose out!" Badger dragged, yanked, ripped at the soaked mane until the horse's muzzle was six inches out of the water. The horse snorted, spraying my face, but I clung on, digging my nails into his throat, anything to keep him from drowning.

Badger went back to get a rope from the boot of the car.

"The daft idiot." His lad appeared on top of the bank, shaken, with blood trickling down his cheek.

"What's his name?" I snapped, urgency cutting through everything.

"Murphy's Law. Murphy for short."

"There we are, Murphy, steady, Murphy, good, Murphy." The bloodshot eyes rolled up at me but the soft words broke through the frenzy. He knew then I was trying to help. He lay very still and blew gently into my hand.

Badger used the rope to haul the trapped hind leg out. It had been rammed against a drainage pipe. The big horse lurched upwards out of the water and staggered on to all four legs. Miraculously, he looked unhurt apart from a few deep thorns which would have to be drawn and poulticed.

I ran my hands down his legs, neck, flanks, my heart skipping beats, feeling the taut muscles, the wall of chest, the powerful hindquarters. I knew something had happened, something I couldn't explain. It was as if in helping this big horse I'd seen inside his soul, what made him tick, his fears, his courage, his guts . . . A bond was there now, as real as a strand of cotton. He breathed on my cheek and whickered as I stepped away. He felt it too – the trust in a human being.

"Stupid big lump." The lad scuffed a clod of soil at the chestnut legs.

"Stop it!" I lunged forward.

"Justina," Badger said, warning me with his eyes to keep out of it.

One of the girls on one of the other horses had more sense. She came and threw a dry quarter sheet over the chestnut's back.

"Thanks." I said it as if he were my horse.

"I can't believe he did that." She had a round face and freckles. "He's not normally so jumpy."

"It was the car horn," I said. "He doesn't like loud noises. He's sensitive like that."

"Right." She looked at me as if nothing would convince her the horse wasn't mad.

Badger watched Murphy and his lad trot off and then said he'd be contacting the small permit trainer, John Robinson, and telling him to keep his string of just-broken racehorses off public roads.

I had to haul myself back into the car and I didn't take my eyes off the chestnut horse until we disappeared round the bend and all I could see was the dense wall of hedge. I couldn't believe he'd jumped it. I vowed I'd come back and measure that hedge, inch for inch.

Badger and I sat in the car drenched and plastered with mud which stuck like glue. I had to keep finding cloths for him to wipe the steering wheel and the gear stick. All I wanted to do was talk about the chestnut horse called Murphy who I was already imagining winning the National before he was even seven years old. Badger had one thought only – Newbury – and turned the radio on full blast for the last race.

"The Guv'nor'll want to see him," I rabbited on, my heart pumping at full speed. "But he'll know he's a champion, it stands out twenty miles."

Badger wasn't listening. He was craning his head to listen to the crackling commentary. I zapped it.

"What did you do that for?" he yelled and flicked it back on.

"And it's Pridwell Pride making all from Shannigan closely followed by Rothwell making a late challenge. And it's two furlongs to go and it's still Pridwell Pride by two lengths . . ."

"You're not listening," I kept one hand over the button so he couldn't turn the volume up again.

"For God's sake. What is it? If it's anything less than appendicitis . . ."

"The chestnut horse," I stammered, adrenalin still rocketing round my body so I had trouble speaking. "We've got to get it to Dolphin Barn. He'll change everything. He's another Aldiniti, Lord Guillene, Corbiere, even, heck, I know it sounds potty, but Red Rum. He'll put Dolphin Barn back on the map. He'll—"

Badger stared at me, open-mouthed and unusually pale. Any longer and he'd start to dribble.

"You're right." He spoke in a high-pitched voice as if he'd swallowed helium. "It is potty. It's the most ridiculous notion I've ever heard. That horse couldn't win a race if it had a twenty furlong head start. It's a boat with four legs. No. Correction. A barge. It needs to be lined up in working hunter classes but don't tell me that's a racehorse – it'd be laughed off the track. Please tell me you're having me on."

I was hurt, physically stung. I grasped the car seat with both hands, weak with shock.

He turned the radio back on but the race was over. A local weather report was on, warning of more cold weather and he growled under his breath.

"Just for the record," I forced out of frozen jaws, "I've never been more serious in my life."

Pridwell Pride and Make Your Own Luck had won for Dolphin Barn. We knew as soon as we drove into the yard. It was written on everybody's faces. For weeks nobody had so much as whistled and now they were grinning like Cheshire cats.

Mandy ran across, popping with the news and forgetting that it wasn't hip to talk to me. "Rory Calligan rode two blinders," she gasped. "The Guv'nor's going doolally. He wants him to ride Tralligan at next week's big race at Kempton."

My blood seemed to pull up short and change direction at a hundred miles an hour. I was Tralligan's lass. I'd be going with them, walking round the parade ring in front of the cameras and rubbing shoulders with Rory. He'd listen with respect as I'd murmur a few words about the horse's character. He'd know me instantly from that day at the racecourse . . .

"And you're so lucky," Mandy yabbered on. "Work ride's gone up for tomorrow and you're schooling fences with Jacko and Rory. He's coming over to see Tralligan for himself and . . ."

I wasn't listening. I was haring towards the hostel and the noticeboard which told us what work was to be done the next day.

Sure enough, there it was, in red pen.

Justina – Leonora.

Jacko – Respect Yourself.

Rory Calligan – Tralligan.

The words tumbled around in my head. I was going to school fences. The Guv'nor thought I was good enough to take Leonora over jumps in front of one of the most famous jockeys in the country. I knew he wanted to prove a point – that he'd been right to take me on. I wouldn't buckle under the pressure. I knew I could come through. I wouldn't let the Guv'nor down. This was the chance I'd been waiting for – for so long.

Four

I was as nervous as a kitten and shaking from hunger, having skipped breakfast. It was like a ritual. Six-thirty, get up. Muck out. Give the horses a dressing over, grooming them, setting their manes and tails right, cleaning their eyes and nostrils and picking out their feet. Then tacking up, simple snaffle bridle and rubber reins. Work saddle over a woolly rug to keep the horses' muscles warm.

Each horse had different work depending on the stage of its training and whether a race was coming up. At first, I'd hacked Leonora out alone for weeks, building up her muscles and hardening her legs. Then I had started canter work upsides another horse, gradually putting more pressure on her to go faster. Now she was like a different horse. The nerves had gone. She was quiet and confident and looked as good as any other horse in the yard.

I took a real pride in doing my two horses and

wisped and brushed them until my whole body ached and their coats gleamed like silk. Looking after racehorses was bliss to me. I was always first on the yard and had finished my chores before anyone else. I know Badger was impressed with my dedication but it wasn't just him I needed to impress. Maybe now the stable's luck had changed, the Guv'nor might send me for my jockey's licence so I could ride Leonora in her first race.

"Good luck." Mandy popped her head over the door, grinning sheepishly. She'd become much more friendly recently. "You're not like the rest of us," she said wistfully. "You're going places."

"Oh I hope so, Mandy, you've no idea how much."

Scooby came out of the hostel singing an old Sinatra song. It was just getting light, there was a thin mist but nothing to worry about. "Here." He whipped a fried egg sandwich out of his bobble hat which he had in his hand. "I know you can't hang on until after first lot. Don't want you collapsing on the Guv'nor."

I tore into the sandwich, grateful to Mandy and Scooby for their support. I was finally starting to make friends. The nagging homesickness was ebbing away like the tide.

Scooby was full of gossip about the night before. All the lads were the worse for wear. They had been celebrating the two wins, but Jacko was particularly bad. Harris had won the prize for the best turned out horse, a whole fresh salmon. After a few drinks the lads had bet Jacko that he couldn't swallow the eye of the salmon, and of course he did and now had a dodgy stomach, which Scooby thought served him right. Jake was still in the suit he'd worn to the races and had been locked out of the hostel as a joke. Chances were he'd have to do work ride in his best pin stripe. The Guv'nor was going to go ballistic because Leonora's owners were coming up from Lambourn and he wanted to set a good impression.

Rory pulled into the yard fifteen minutes before we were due on the gallops. He had an old coat pulled over breeches and chaps and he still looked drop-dead gorgeous.

I was annoyed with myself for turning to jelly and tried to look busy, but it was impossible when he let a spotted Great Dane unfold itself out of the back of the car. Mandy and Shona melted with lots of oohs and aahs.

"This is Poppy." Rory scratched the huge dog's ears. "The only girl in my life."

I realized that I was staring over the stable door like an imbecile and turned abruptly to pick out Leonora's hooves for the sixth time. Secretly I was impressed that he loved animals and that he had a normal car with a scruffy backseat.

The Guv'nor came out of the house with a

smart couple who must have been Leonora's owners. It was them more than anybody who sent my heart catapulting against my ribcage. I was on trial, there was nothing more sure. With sweating palms I led Tralligan out of his stable and tightened the girth, avoiding his snapping jaws. Rory walked across, unruffled and easy, drinking in the horse, learning all he could.

I waited. He smiled politely and took up the reins, expecting me to leg him up. He hadn't recognized me. The realization bit into my feelings. I was more hurt than I could say. What had I expected? An embrace, a joke, a friendly grin. I fumbled with his leg, feeling the colour scorch up my neck.

Jacko staggered out of the hostel clutching his skull cap and looking jaundiced. This was going to be eventful. You could practically touch the rivalry between us.

Chelsea growled ferociously at the sight of another dog and sent Poppy gangling across the cobbles looking for Rory. In panic she shot straight between my legs and nearly lifted me off my feet.

"You riding that today?" Jacko mocked, never missing a put-down. He was riding Respect Yourself, or Dobby as he was called in the stable.

"I'll show him," I thought, confidence flooding back as I mounted Leonora.

Up on the gallops we split up, Rory going

towards the steeplechase fences and Jacko and myself towards the hurdles. It was the first time Leonora had seen fences and it was important to have a lead from an older horse. Dobby was an experienced hurdler, getting ready for the switch to steeplechasing.

"Justina," the Guv'nor shouted, "stay upsides Jacko. Give the mare a good ride."

I bridged my reins for a better grip as we cantered down to the first flight of hurdles. Leonora's owners had their binoculars glued on my back. I wasn't going to get away with the slightest mistake. The mare's eyes goggled as I showed her the first hurdle. Jacko was no help at all, he just kept his mouth clamped shut and turned the colour of mushy peas.

The Guv'nor gave the sign and we circled and turned off, gathering speed. The rush of air and the pounding hooves soon washed away any nerves. I could feel my face splitting into a grin. The first hurdle flashed by, it was over before Leonora realized it was there. She cat-leapt the first two, then settled into a rhythm and started taking them in her stride. She was a natural, as light on her feet as a ballerina. I kept myself tucked in and tidy, going with the movement. A rider left behind at this stage could seriously dent a horse's confidence.

It suddenly occurred to me that we were going hell for leather. This wasn't a three quarter gallop, it was suicidal. What was Jacko playing at? I tried to shout across but he just drew further away. After the last hurdle I pulled up and watched Dobby disappear into some trees and streak out of the other side. It was ages before Jacko managed to pull him up.

I walked back to the Guv'nor expecting a rollicking for going so fast but the only one talking was the owner's wife who was singing the virtues of female jockeys. I wanted to kiss her when she hounded the Guv'nor about letting me race ride. She wanted me to ride Leonora!

Jacko came back red in the face and cursing. "Why did you keep on my tail?" he yelled in front of everyone. "Can't you see when someone's getting run off with?"

My esteem shrank to the size of a pea. The last thing a runaway horse needed was another horse running upsides encouraging it to keep going. But, even so, I was pretty sure Jacko had deliberately started off too fast to scare me. It was his fault he'd lost control. The Guv'nor said nothing, which meant he probably thought the same thing.

I was later to find out from Scooby that Jacko had got off behind some trees, been sick, and then hopped back on from an old farm implement.

While all this was going on Rory was cruising round the steeplechase fences looking every inch a champion and making Tralligan look a better horse than he actually was. My mouth dropped open with admiration. Television never gets across the level of skill and technique – it was all so smooth and balanced with Rory finding the right stride again and again.

Meanwhile, Jacko looked as if he was going to die when the Guv'nor ordered him to do a line of steeplechase fences. Dobby thought his work was done for the day and tried to roll. He crashed through three of the fences and only just skimmed over the last. Rory was walking Tralligan back on a loose rein, his body moving easily with the long strides. He looked as if he'd been born on the back of a horse.

Jacko was floundering. The Guv'nor asked him to do one fence back to front to sharpen up the old rogue. Jacko was horrified. He started babbling and backtracking with every excuse under the sun.

"I'll do it, Guv'nor." The words flew out of my mouth of their own accord. Before I knew what was what I was swapping horses.

Rory suddenly noticed me, and became alert with interest. I couldn't stuff up now. Not with his gorgeous brown eyes focused on my performance. I kicked Dobby forward and tried to instill in him that I was having no nonsense.

Jumping a fence backwards is an old trainer's trick to get a horse to lift himself more. He can't sweep through the birch as he usually would – he has to come up in front, really put in an effort. I was still flying high in the knowledge that Jacko was too scared to do it and so all eyes were on me. This was my chance. I took a deep breath, urging the horse into a canter. I couldn't hear anything but the frantic heartbeats inside my chest. I chose the highest schooling fence with the worst take off.

"Hold your nerve, hold your nerve." The fence loomed up. Dobby was galloping well but not seriously imagining I'd ask him to do the jump ahead. When I rode at it like an arrow he goggled and panicked. I closed my hands and legs, willing him to have confidence in me. Hold or lengthen? I made a split-second decision and Dobby put in the biggest jump, probably of his whole life.

A huge smile broke out inside me as I headed back towards the Guv'nor's group. Wear that, everyone, I grinned, wanting to punch the air. The Guv'nor looked slightly shell-shocked. Mrs Jennings, Leonora's owner, was talking ten to the dozen and Jacko was glowering like a bull, well and truly put in his place.

But I was interested only in Rory's reaction. Deliberately casually, I glanced across, aching for his approval. He was smirking, highly amused. But he was impressed, I could see it in his eyes. He wouldn't forget me again. Not in a hurry anyway.

It wasn't just the buzz of riding racehorses that kept me wide awake that night in bed. It wasn't just the warm cosy sensation every time I replayed the events of the day. It was something I would never admit to anyone, not even Mandy or Scooby. I was falling hopelessly in love with Rory Calligan.

Five

I had no idea that my life was going to take a turn for the worse. The lads at the stables were specially nice after my riding feat on Dobby. Even respectful. I always got warm chips in the canteen now and no more leg-pulling about Bumper Velvet. Mandy latched on to me like a barnacle with a touch of hero worship. Shona still sizzled and spat in the corner but I could live with her. She was jealous sick of my new-found popularity.

A couple of weeks later, a virus hit me so hard I could barely get out of bed. I was sweating buckets and had to suffer the embarrassment of the Guv'nor coming up the stairs and seeing me in my nightshirt. Even Smokey found me too clingy and forlorn and scarpered.

I went into mourning when the Guv'nor left. He was sending me home. He said I was too ill to be Tralligan's lass in Rory's next race, and he couldn't risk all his staff being infected. It was the only sensible option. Think of it like a horse being quarantined, he said. I'd have other chances – he was sure of it.

I wanted to bawl my eyes out. It wasn't just missing my first big race! It was missing the chance to be next to Rory, to lead him round the paddock on Tralligan, talk to him intimately, be right there with him. I'd dreamt of nothing else since he'd seen me on Dobby. I'd imagined every scenario, from him hugging me in the winner's enclosure to him running after me and asking, no, begging, for a date.

I was distraught. If I'd been homesick when I'd first arrived I now felt inseparable from Dolphin Barn. Take away the horses, the fresh early mornings, the gossip and laughs, the racing talk from morning till night, even the cruel teasing, and I'd be like a fish on dry land gasping for its last breath.

I didn't feel any better when Mandy and Scooby gave me a framed picture of me riding Leonora which Mrs Jennings had taken without me knowing. My heart skipped when I saw Rory in the background.

Mum picked me up, hope flickering in her eyes that they'd worked me to death and I'd had enough. It faded when I left a load of Polo mints in Scooby's care, a packet for each horse.

My time at home was quiet and formal. Mum and Dad purposefully avoided talking about racing and I spent all day playing with my twin brothers who I truly had missed.

I watched Rory's race on telly. I was so excited, I perched on the edge of the coffee table so I could get a good view. By the time I saw Jake walking Tralligan round the parade ring, tears were streaming down my face.

"Dustbin?" The twins, who couldn't pronounce Justina, pulled at my sleeves, worried that I was upset.

Rory looked spectacular in blue and orange diamond silks, although I could tell he was nervous. Tralligan started 16 to 1 and I had everything crossed apart from my eyes. If Dolphin Barn could win this race . . .

Kempton was a fast three miles on a flat track but I knew Tralligan could do it. There were only three horses in the race. Nobody made the running to start with and they took the fifth fence from home abreast. And then, suddenly, Rory pressed the right buttons and Tralligan shot ahead, running gallantly on to win by three lengths.

"Justina, whatever's the matter?" Mum came in carrying a box of Thorntons chocolates. I was sobbing my heart out, drenching a velvet cushion which I'd been clutching for the last two minutes. "We've won, Mum," I wailed. "Isn't it fantastic!"

Then I sat transfixed. Rory was being interviewed. If the video had packed up at that moment I'd have needed psychiatric care.

My high that night was wrenched away from me the next day. I felt as if I'd been swallowed up in an earthquake.

As I had done since my childhood, I opened *The Racing Post* at the results page. Scanning down, my heart stood still when I saw Murphy's Law pulled up in a seller at Nottingham. A seller is a race at which the horses are for sale. Chestnut. Five years old. No form to date. It had to be him.

But the shock really hit home in the next race down. Leonora ridden by claiming jockey Jack Hughes . . . fell at the last . . .

I was frozen with hurt. The Guv'nor had run Leonora behind my back, and with my worst enemy on board. Before she was ready. How could he have done that to me?

I sat motionless for the best part of an hour, numb with shock. I could never go back to ride at Dolphin Barn now. I felt cheated and trodden on and used.

The Guv'nor wasn't going to get away with it.

"How could you do that?" I marched up and down in the office, even more hurt and upset after seeing Leonora on edge and tense, all my good work down the drain. "I want to resign." My voice came out small, even though inside my whole body was screaming.

"I won't accept," the Guv'nor snapped, his face shut down and stubborn. "I know this is a shattering blow."

"You don't know anything," I yelled. "If you did, you'd give me a chance instead of favouring fools like Jacko. I've worked my heart out for you and all you do is treat me like dirt."

"That's enough." He leapt up, gripping the table. "If it was anyone else, I'd send them packing right now."

I flopped down in the chair, tears forcing their way out. I was spent. I still didn't feel well and there was no more fight in me.

"Who pays for this whole operation, Justina, have you ever considered that?"

I kept my head down. It was like being back at school.

"Owners, that's who. Owners. Every time. And I have to dance on water to keep each one happy. Otherwise they take horses away and I can't pay wages. That's the reality, Justina. And if an owner insists on running their horse so they can show off to the relatives then that's how it's got to be. I can advise and steer but at the end of the day, it's their horse. They call the shots."

He sat down heavily, wearily, and for the first time I saw the real man behind the armour plating. I was shocked by what he'd said. I'd never considered the pressure he was under from the people who owned the horses, their whims, their expectations, their disappointments. I vowed that if I ever became a trainer, the horses would come first, always.

"Yes, Mrs Jennings wanted you to ride Leonora, but she wanted Leonora to run even more and you were sick. I had no choice. You're a good jockey, Justina. You might even be brilliant. But it's not going to be easy. And it's not going to happen overnight."

A flood of warmth washed over me. It was unheard of for the Guv'nor to give praise, he'd told me so himself on my first morning out. He'd never told me I could be good. My spirits lifted to the roof. I even patted Chelsea, who nearly took my fingers off. All thoughts of resignation were gone.

"Here, this might make you feel better." He flicked across an application form which I grabbed before it sailed to the floor. At the top he'd filled in a blank box. "Miss Justina Margaret Brooks." It was for a jockey's licence.

"Everything's coming up worms." Scooby put his hands in the air in despair because Tralligan had a "bit of a leg" after his last race.

Most racehorses had leg problems from injuries or strain and it wasn't uncommon to go into a yard and see nothing but bandaged patients. I had to cold-hose him down three times a day and keep him poulticed. He was in a filthy mood because

43

he couldn't go out of his stable and started dunking his nose in the automatic waterer and blowing bubbles to amuse himself.

My main worry was Leonora. Her confidence was shattered. She was back to square one. A thin weal on her left side made me boil with anger. She'd had the whip and lots of it. I could have taken a birch to Jacko.

"What did you think you were doing, using the whip on such a nervous horse in her first race?" I yelled at him in the yard later that day.

"If it's any of your business, Bumper Velvet," Jacko sneered, "I was keeping her straight on the run home. Even a schoolgirl knows that a taste of the whip keeps a tired horse from drifting, and she was tired, thanks to your training methods."

"Yeah? Well, even a schoolgirl knows that there's no sense in whacking a horse after it's already given its best," I snapped. "What were you trying to do? Put her off racing for the rest of her life?"

He just shrugged and turned away.

"It's people like you who make decent people call for the whip to be banned. You're nothing but a bully and a disgrace to racing," I called after his retreating back.

I bathed Leonora's cut with witch hazel and tried to reassure her with love and care. She turned her back on me and stared at the wall, and I knew that she was angry that I'd deserted her when she needed me most.

If I was ever to beat the top male jockeys I had to get inside a horse's head, just as I had with Murphy that day. We had to share the same skin. It was always said that a man would beat a woman any day on a run-in because of his superior strength, but I knew that understanding the horse was what would give the edge.

If I couldn't bully my horses to win races, I had to persuade them to want to win, to be on my side. I had to learn how to be a horse's friend from the very first moment. I had to develop a sixth sense with every mount.

The Gov'nor was obviously still trying to make things up to me because the next day I was sent on a buying trip with Badger.

It was just what I needed. We piled into the horsebox, me clutching the sales catalogue which was the size of a doorstop. Badger had instructions to buy a promising five year old with a bit of form to go hurdling for a new client. The Guv'nor had marked the horses he wanted us to look at and given Badger a price scale, which he kept to himself.

There were hundreds and hundreds of horses in the catalogue and I skimmed them with an eagle eye, soaking up the bloodlines and form. I picked out a string of chasers which I'd have bought if I had a fortune in the bank. I couldn't get there quickly enough. By the time we arrived, Badger and I weren't talking because we couldn't agree on the name of the fifty-one-year-old grandmother who'd finished fifth in the '94 National.

We parked the box and headed straight to the stables in sloshing rain to view our first prospective horse. Each entry was led out for examination with a number on its rump.

It was all very organized, with loads of buyers walking up and down the aisles scribbling things in their catalogues. The first horse Badger asked to see was a light-framed black gelding with a white star. Badger walked round and round sucking in his cheeks, deep in thought. I was dying to know what he was thinking but I'd had strict instructions not to look interested. If it got back to the auctioneer, the price could be sent sky-high by a runner, or artificial buyer, making false bids. It probably explained why everybody was walking round sour-faced and shaking their heads.

The next three horses all had things wrong with them, sickle hocks, flat feet, straight shoulders, long backs. Badger and the Guv'nor insisted that no matter how well-bred a horse, it still had to have quality and good conformation. By the seventh horse I was shaking my head and scouring for defects just like everyone else.

Badger was finishing off with a couple of tail-enders while I went to find some refreshments. It was as I was cutting through one of the barns with stabling inside that I saw him. Murphy's Law. He was standing at the back of his stable, which was flooded from a blocked drain. He was tied up on a short chain and he looked utterly miserable.

I was in the stable like a shot, running my hands all over him, feeling the familiar magic. We had to take him back to Dolphin Barn. We had to. Murphy was a horse I could understand, but somehow I had to convince Badger. With shaking fingers I flicked through the catalogue to his number. It was right at the back. Irish bred out of a little known stallion. 17.1 hands. Box walker. That meant he wouldn't fetch very much money.

I was shaking all over now. What I was about to do might lose me my job but I had to go through with it. I kissed his velvety, soft nose, trying to reassure him that he was going to be all right. He gave me a wink with one of his sweet, sensitive eyes and I knew he understood.

I met Badger in the sales ring and passed him a polystyrene cup of hot coffee. Mine had sloshed all down my front but he didn't seem to notice that, nor that my teeth were chattering and I kept glancing wildly around.

The atmosphere was electric as the big hitters were auctioned off first. One horse fetched over twenty thousand guineas. The horses paraded below while the auctioneer rat-tatted out his spiel. It was infectious, the bids came thick and fast, half unseen, as the auctioneer wooed the punters to part with their money, spiralling the price up and whipping the bidders into a heady whirl of excitement.

I sat on my hands until they turned numb. Waves of sickness erupted from my stomach at the thought of what I was about to do. Badger blew through his teeth when the black gelding made twice what he bid. I knew there was only one other horse he really fancied. Half the racing population of England and Ireland seemed to have turned out on this miserable, wet afternoon.

I was sitting halfway up the tiers looking down on the range of bidders. Some had mobile phones, some were frantically writing in their catalogues, and others were packing up and going home, disappointed at the day's outcome.

The sale was coming to a close. Badger was hanging on for a leggy filly, his last interest. I shut down like a clam as Murphy's Law was led into the ring. Nobody else seemed to notice. He walked clumsily, scared of the noise and lights. Badger stirred as if he recollected something, but then his own phone rang and he was distracted.

The auctioneer started his patter without much enthusiasm. A lady in the first row made a bid with her rolled-up catalogue.

"Come on, ladies and gentlemen, don't let a big

powerful chasing type like this get away from you. A few more years and we'll have the model of Burrough Hill Lad. Now come on, do I hear seven hundred guineas? Seven hundred. Seven hundred and fifty? Any advance on seven hundred and fifty guineas?"

The bidding stopped as the auctioneer scanned the tiers, stroking his gavel. He looked bored, wanting to wind things up. Murphy stopped, rooted to the spot, and wouldn't move.

There was a snigger round the ring and the woman in front shook her head. This was the moment. A fraction too late and it would all be over. I threw up my hand, and my whole body followed so I was the only one standing up in the tiers. My voice came out thick and unrecognizable. I yelled out, "Eight hundred guineas!" as loudly as I could, and heard the hushed whispers all around.

The gavel came crashing down as the auctioneer sensed my urgency and clinched the deal. Badger froze next to me. His mobile phone clattered to the ground. He started breathing shallowly as if he had asthma. Murphy was shooed out of the ring in a rush and another horse immediately led in. I didn't wait a second longer. I flew out, into the pouring rain, gagging for breath. I couldn't really believe what I'd done or the enormity of the consequences.

The rain washed down my face, cooling my

panic. I heard footsteps behind me and Badger hauled me round, gripping my left shoulder and pressing down hard.

I'd never seen anger like his. I'd once heard of a savage racehorse who used to throw himself down on his knees and bite the ground in a temper and this is almost what I expected Badger to do now. He looked as if he could have ripped my head open in one go.

"Aaagh, what's the use? The Guv'nor'll deal with yer. Yer his responsibility, not mine. But Lord knows he'll be the laughing stock this time."

We travelled home in silence, Badger hissing through his teeth and Murphy tied up in the back. I'd got what I wanted, so why did I feel my heart sinking?

Everyone at Dolphin came out to see the new horse. It was always like that, no matter how many horses we had in training, it always created a wave when another one arrived.

Murphy wouldn't come out of the horsebox. I had to coax and cajole him for fifteen minutes and then he rocketed down the ramp and fell on his knees. I didn't have to look at everyone's faces, I could feel the disappointment. Jacko, Steve and Harris hung round, sensing a scene.

I led Murphy into the newly made-up stable but I'd no sooner unclipped the lead rope than he barged past me and started marching round and round the four walls, knocking his head on the rough brick, going faster and faster. By the time the Guv'nor and Badger arrived he was drenched in sweat and attempting to canter in his stable.

The catalogue had been right. He was a box walker. I burst into tears.

The Guv'nor glanced over the door, rigid with disbelief. "Oh, my girl," he whispered, as if he had a hairball stuck in his throat. "What have you done?"

Six

It was decided that Murphy would be put straight back in the next available sale. That meant I had six weeks to convince the Guv'nor he had a champion on his hands and not a donkey.

Every moment I had was wrapped up in Murphy. The first thing I had to sort out was his box walking. It was quite clear that he'd never make a racehorse while he wore himself to a rag pacing his stable. But how to do it? I tried everything, lifting his bedding, closing the top door, changing his feed, putting him in a larger stable, a smaller stable. I even tried tying him up but he fretted and sweated and wore himself out day after day.

I was running out of time. Everyone I spoke to said that box walking was a vice like crib biting and there was no cure. In the end Murphy was put in the isolation unit so the other horses wouldn't copy him. I was starting to despair.

Everyone tormented me endlessly. It was hopeless. I was the butt of every joke. It was like my early days at Dolphin Barn all over again. All the respect I'd finally earned was gone.

"He looks better today." Mandy tried to cheer me up. She'd brought me a banana and a tomato sandwich because I'd started to avoid the canteen. I had booted Murphy's legs up so he wouldn't hurt himself. He looked like a baseball player. Mandy surveyed him for a few moments, munching on a ham roll. She was a good-hearted girl who hated to see anyone unhappy. "Maybe he's lonely," she said, out of the blue.

"My God, that's it!" I screeched, wanting to kiss her. It was so obvious. Why hadn't I thought of it? I dashed into the hostel and ripped a local newspaper out of one of the lad's hands. I was trembling as I scoured the adverts.

"Look here," Jacko sneered. "Calamity Jane's tracking down another racehorse. Must be that Shire we saw last week, Steve. Been in touch with Mystic Meg have yer, luv?" He stuck out a leg so I tripped on my way to the pay phone, but his taunting didn't have the slightest effect. I scrabbled in my pocket for a twenty pence coin and dialled the number.

It was late that afternoon when the small pig trailer rattled into the yard and a red-faced farmer wearing a flat cap got out of the pick-up and lowered the ramp. I paid him what we had agreed and he drove off leaving me holding a frayed rope attached to a small goat with beady eyes. My confidence didn't soar when it butted me three times in the back of the knees en route to Murphy's stable.

This was my final hope. I dragged the goat through the door and stood back to watch. Murphy's eyes nearly popped out of his head. He snorted and stared for long minutes and when I'd convinced myself that he wasn't going to hurt it I locked them in and left them to it.

An hour later they were eating together like long-lost buddies and Murphy had stopped box walking. I put my hands over my face and wept with relief. I could now start the difficult job of training him.

If I'd taken stick before from the lads it was nothing like what I now got about Gertie the goat. Every other day I'd go into the stable and she'd be dressed up in a pair of antlers or a Superman cloak. Steve got extra brave one day and kidnapped her. Murphy went beserk and cut his leg so badly he was off work for a week. I got my own back by pinching Steve's underwear and hanging it from the clock tower above the stable yard.

The downside of a horse who has a goat for a best friend is that Gertie had to tag along everywhere. This was particularly embarrassing up on the gallops, especially when owners turned up to watch their horses. I quickly worked out that because Murphy was so big, he hadn't found his natural balance. He was like a gawky teenager who didn't quite know what to do with himself. Ask him to canter and he plaited his legs and nearly fell on his nose. It wasn't that he couldn't canter, he just didn't know how.

Every night I'd switch the lights on in the indoor school and lunge him, with Gertie tied up in the corner. As he circled on the end of the long line he often stumbled, and twice fell, but gradually he worked out how to shift his weight back on to his quarters and lighten his forelegs. After a couple of weeks I introduced trotting poles and small jumps. In showjumping and eventing, hours and hours are spent teaching horses technique, yet in racing, if a horse isn't a natural from the word go, he tends to get pushed to the bottom of the pile.

By putting a placing pole in front of a jump as a marker for him, I could ensure that Murphy would meet it just right. Every day his confidence grew and it wasn't long before he was learning to judge distances for himself.

The gruelling hours were taking their toll. I was exhausted and kept catching every infection known to man. One night when my chest was particularly bad and I was rasping and wheezing in front of the telly, Mandy decided to treat me to a home-cooked meal. She said afterwards it was lasagne but at the time it tasted more like a rubber tyre. I dutifully grappled with every mouthful and then dowsed the taste with a dose of Lemsip. There was a programme on television I was aching to watch which meant I had to switch all the lights off and sit very still, otherwise the picture turned into a snowstorm. It was called *Ride to Fall* and it featured young jockeys in the high-risk sport of jump racing. I hadn't seen Rory since that day on the gallops when we schooled over fences, but twenty-four hours didn't pass without me conjuring up his face and engaging him in imaginary conversations.

When his profile came up next to Dougie Barnes and Liam O'Riley, I nearly fell out of my chair. He'd had his hair cropped short and looked even more gorgeous than ever. The interviewer asked him loads of personal questions and an embarrassed blush fired up his neck. When she asked about girlfriends, he changed the subject.

"You fancy him!" Mandy walked in, nursing Smokey and staring at me accusingly. Heaven knows how long she'd been hovering in the shadows watching my expression. The telly immediately turned to a white fuzz.

"Look what you've done. Move!" The withdrawal effects were terrible.

"Well?" Mandy had her hand on her hip, puckering her lips, in a tell-me-now stance.

"You've got it all wrong," I bluffed. "I only admire his riding, that's what I'm in love with."

"Oh, thank heavens for that." She plopped down heavily in the opposite chair, still squeezing the life out of poor Smokey. "For a minute there I thought I had serious competition."

"Justina, leave it alone, will you, for heaven's sake. The horse is going back in the sales and that's the end of it." The Guv'nor unwrapped a green jumper his sister had knitted for him and scowled in distaste. Green was his unlucky colour.

I wouldn't give up. "But you can't. He'll win everything for you. You've got to give him a chance."

The Guv'nor had turned red in the face. He ordered me out of the office.

"He's capable of anything," I protested. "You haven't even seen him work. How professional is that? You're so set in your ways you won't even wear a green jumper."

I thought he was going to explode, but miraculously I got what I wanted. There were two weeks before the next sale and the Guv'nor was giving me till then to prove that Murphy was as good as I claimed.

"Have you heard?" Mandy rushed into the cottage kitchen, ignoring the pile of pots and her name beside "washing-up" on the rota. "Rory's

57

going to be the new stable jockey, starting today. Isn't that fantastic? I'll be able to see him all the time." She lowered her voice as Shona shimmied down the stairs, wearing heavy-duty lipstick and skin-tight jodphurs.

I nodded dully, numb with nerves. It was glaringly obvious that Mandy and Shona were walking around hoping to be picked up by Rory for a hot date. Mandy grated on about nothing for an eternity and I clenched my jaw, trying desperately not to snap. In the end I grabbed my crash hat and backed soundlessly out of the door.

I kept Murphy at the back of the string of horses and stayed well away from Rory, who was joking casually with Shona. Mandy rode on ahead looking on the brink of tears. Scooby glanced back, giving me the thumbs up sign, but it was all wrong. I usually worked Murphy on his own. Now, as part of a string for the first time, he was boiling over, fretting with excitement and burning off valuable energy. To make matters worse, the Guv'nor was pointedly wearing the green jumper.

The horses circled in the dip, walking and trotting to warm up. There was the usual banter and joking but each pair of eyes kept swinging back to Murphy. "C'mon, c'mon." I keyed myself up, willing both of us to perform. "Find a spark, a turn of foot, don't let him down."

Badger called Rory and me in. Rory was

focused on the job in hand, and barely raised a smile. The bay skittered underneath him but he didn't seem to notice. He flowed with a horse, more like a centaur than a human.

"Build up to a stiff piece of work on the all-weather course and then veer off and take in the hurdles," Badger clipped.

"C'mon, Murphy, do your best." I put my bare hand on his neck and felt the special rapport. He'd run his heart out for me and more.

Both horses surged forward together, matching strides, but only for two furlongs. Murphy refused to settle upsides. He grabbed the bit and towed me to the front. There wasn't anything I could do – my arms might as well have been strings of spaghetti. Every pore in Murphy's body oozed a competitive edge. He'd die rather than be beaten. His big, chestnut ears flapped back whenever the bay drew closer, but it didn't happen more than twice. Murphy was intimidating the other. We tore up the incline, streaking round the edge of the hill.

Rory's horse was left standing by the big chestnut's loping stride. I veered off just in time to line up for the hurdles. I sat still and let the first flimsy barrier come to us. Murphy flew over it, gaining speed in the air. Surely the Guv'nor had to see his talent. We rocketed the next three and turned slightly downhill for the last. I had to shorten him. I hooked back the reins and asked for an extra stride. It didn't work. Murphy's head came up fast and he practically lurched to a standstill. Then he dived upwards, legs splaying in all directions. He didn't make it. He clipped the top of the hurdle and somersaulted badly.

For the next few seconds I was sliding across the turf in a daze. I felt a sickening thud vibrate through the ground as Murphy fell. He shouldn't have fallen, it was my fault. I rolled in a ball towards the wing and then I glanced up. Murphy was down and he wasn't moving.

I stood up swaying, with a taste of sickness in my throat. If he was dead . . . People were running from all directions. His eyes stared blankly into space and his breath rasped away like someone sawing wood.

"Get his saddle off quick." The Guv'nor took charge.

"The blooming idiot landed on his head." Badger tried to be angry to hide his feelings.

"A broken neck," I heard someone murmur.

"No, he wouldn't still be alive."

"Will you shut up," I whirled round, manic with grief.

Despite all the men, I pushed through and clung to Murphy's head, stroking the sweat out of his eyes.

"Get the girl away . . ."

"We've rung the vet. He's just setting off now."

"Better get the other horses back to the yard."

I let them all take charge. I just nursed my horse and tried to make him better. Time seemed to stand still.

"The vet's just turned in, Guv."

"Right, let's clear the site."

I felt hands slip under my armpits and hoist me up. "No. Leave me alone!" But my strength was sapping and I let Rory lead me away, burying my head in his jacket. I never wanted to go near a horse again. Not after this.

"Hey, Guv, he's getting up!"

I snapped my head round to see Murphy sitting on his haunches and then pulling himself up with a groan.

"He's up, he's OK!" Badger was grasping the bridle.

I stumbled forward but my legs wouldn't function. Rory was there instantly with a supporting arm. Hot salty tears ran into my mouth.

He was OK. Badger led him forward, but there wasn't a mark on him. He was like a cat with nine lives. He even yawned, showing yellow teeth, and stretched as if he'd been having forty winks. I rested my head on his shoulder and felt the familiar chestnut nose rustle my pockets.

The vet listened to his heart and lungs and pulled up the lids of his eyes. Normal. "Must have been winded. Box rest for a few days and careful observation." The vet shook his head in wonder.

I knew then that Murphy was lucky to be alive.

"Never ever take a pull so close to a fence. Is that clear?" The Guv'nor was blowing through his teeth like a horse and shredding a piece of paper without noticing. "It was the worst display of jockeymanship I've ever seen." The scant hairs on the side of his temples stood up in a current of static. "I want to run him in the Wilcow Hurdle at Chepstow." He suddenly changed direction.

"W-what?" I blanched.

"Rory can ride him. Let's see what he can do with a pro on his back."

A laser of jealousy bore into my chest. He then described the type of race that Rory would ride and my throat became drier than a desert. My legs trembled. I knew deep in my gut that it was all wrong. It could only end in disaster . . .

Seven

"It's all wrong!" I tried to stir the baked beans but they'd welded to the pan. The lads would be back any minute from first lot and I was helping Scooby get some food ready for them. "Murphy needs a marathon where he can lead from the front. This race is too short. And Chepstow's a right-handed track and Murphy jumps to the left!"

"So you've told me a hundred times." Scooby turned the bacon.

"But nobody listens," I wailed. "Everyone says it's my hormones or that time of the month. I know what I'm talking about."

Scooby gave me a dark look. I howled in frustration and pinched a fried egg sarnie.

Outside Murphy was surveying the yard from his stable. All the attention that he'd received after the fall had brought him out of his shell. It was as if the farrier had fitted him with platform shoes. He felt noticed and important. I fed him Polo mints and watched his ears waft like antennae. He was sneaking his way into everybody's hearts with his smiley face and endless gratitude. He wasn't like a racehorse at all, but a big mongrel dog who'd been dumped and had then found a good home. It wasn't my imagination, he really was turning from a frog into a prince.

"What do you think?" Mandy did a twirl in a pink cashmere jumper she'd bought from the market.

"Isn't it a bit tight?" I scowled, knowing it was two sizes too small because I'd checked the label earlier.

"That's the idea," she pouted, exasperated. "So it shows off my shape."

It could mean only one thing. Rory was heading for Dolphin Barn at this moment.

"Well, you're just as bad." Mandy admired herself in a compact mirror. "I saw that box of dog biscuits you bought. Wouldn't be for a certain dog called Poppy, would they?" I blushed bright red.

Rory was riding record winners for Dolphin Barn. All the lads had money to burn from backing the horses and so were out every night, but I refused to bet and so did Mandy. We stayed in every night with a pizza and a bottle of Coke.

I ached for my first race more than anything. It was the lifestyle I wanted, the uncertainty, the danger, the ecstasy. The months were slipping away and I still hadn't pulled on my first set of silks. Bruce Hobbs, in 1938, had won the Grand National at seventeen on Battleship. I was being eaten away by frustration.

Sure enough, Rory pulled into the yard before long. Mandy had strategically positioned herself on the drive, sweeping up imaginary hay. It was my afternoon off and Scooby had advised that I get a life and go into Cheltenham. Instead, I offered to take Poppy for a walk and felt like a kid when Rory said he'd pay me.

The yard was empty when I got back. I was frozen to the bone and in a bad mood because Poppy had run off chasing rabbits. I now had her firmly on the lead and dragged her purposefully towards the tack room. Nobody heard me walk in.

Rory had his jersey off, pointing to a livid bruise. "And if you think that's bad, check out this." He pulled down his jods to his hip and pointed to a white, ragged-edged scar.

"Well, I can do better than that." Shona, who was flirting for England, had her jumper rolled up to her bra in no time. "That's where a horse bit me. Can you see the row of stitches?" Her eyes were shining and the sexual chemistry was bouncing off the walls. Desolation washed over me. It was obvious what was going on. The papers were right, Rory charmed girls like he did horses. Why had I thought I was so special?

I slunk out like a whipped puppy and vowed I must never reveal my true feelings to Rory Calligan. Never. Ever. I would rather die in a tower with no food or water, overrun with rats, than let him think I fancied him. I ran full pelt to the cottage and cried all over Smokey, who brushed against my face until cat hairs stuck all down my cheeks.

"Blooming 'eck, what's this, the cabaret show?" Mr Chips, so-called because he was always stopping off at takeaways, couldn't quite believe it when Gertie the goat stepped up the horsebox ramp ahead of Murphy, in a miniature blue-and-silver travelling rug. Mr Chips drove the racehorses all over the country and changed gears as if he was carrying explosives. He always had a thermos flask on the dashboard, and a china cup and saucer. Scooby said he hadn't spilt a drop in twenty years, not even on the M25. He was taking us to Chepstow.

Murphy blundered in after Gertie and stood in line next to the other horses. The lads piled into the living accommodation of the vehicle and settled down to do crosswords, play cards or catch up on sleep.

The other travelling head lad, Scottie, who lived on his nerves, sat next to Mr Chips, rummaging through the passes for the horses and the stable lads. There was so much paperwork, especially if the horses were staying overnight. If a flu jab had been overlooked or a horse hadn't been declared, it could be a long trip home. The travelling head lad also had to collect all the appropriate silks from the office and check they belonged to the right owner. Jake, one of the other lads, was moaning because his horse's owner favoured shocking pink hoops.

My stomach churned as the portable steps were pulled in. Jake amused himself making aeroplanes out of paper napkins and aiming them at Scottie through the interior door. Everyone was trying to decide where to lay bets. One lad, Roy, nicknamed Roy Rogers because he'd never been near a horse until he started at racing college, said his money was riding on Gertie in the 3.10. Nobody was putting a bean on Murphy. They were all convinced he would fall at the first.

I couldn't stand it. I zipped down the passage to be near the horses. I was shaking all over. I had to pull myself together or Murphy would get the jitters. He watched me with big, soft eyes, and then snorted hay seeds down my neck.

The racecourse was already milling with people. Mr Chips drove round to the stables, where security was tight as ever, and we unloaded the horses and Gertie, who had chewed through her rope.

Murphy was in the second race so I didn't have

much time. One of the plaits in his mane had come loose and Gertie had chewed the end of his tail, which now hung above his hocks.

I had to get a grip. Breathe slowly. Relax. Roy Rogers had a bay mare in the same race so I could copy him to an extent. At the moment, he was chatting idly to other lads and rolling a prohibited cigarette.

I checked out the pre-parade ring and saddling stalls so I wouldn't get lost. There was a wave of anticipation and excitement, a pre-race buzz, but it wasn't catching – I felt like the only person at a funeral ceremony.

"Hey, Justina." Roy Rogers caught up, over-loaded with number cloths and surcingles. "You're 'just in time' to tack up my horse." He sniggered at his own joke and plonked the gear at my feet. "Got a bit of business on, see you in a jiff."

"Roy!"

Murphy wouldn't open his mouth for the bit. I ended up yelling at him, which made him sulk and blow up his gut so I couldn't tighten the surcingle. When Roy came back I tried to slap him round the head, but he ducked like a boxer.

"Here, I've brought you a Mars Bar, thought your sugar levels might be low."

The last thing I could do was eat so, thinking I was being kind, I screwed off the wrapper and offered it to the bay mare.

"Are you crazy?" Roy knocked it out of my hand, jarring my wrist. "Do you want her to fail a dope test?"

"I'm sorry, Roy," I gasped, appalled at my ignorance. I had so much to learn. I trembled to think how close I'd come to being sacked. "Thanks." I pecked him on the cheek.

"You *do* know that you've put the number cloth on upside down?"

Murphy strode out into the pre-parade ring, neighing every fifteen seconds to a demented Gertie who'd been locked in the stable out of harm's way. I'd spilt hoof oil down my white shirt and had had to borrow Mr Chips's cardigan to cover the stain.

The Guv'nor arrived with the saddles ready and we dived into a spare stall, where Murphy started bucking with the joys of life.

"The going's good to soft. With any luck he should be in with a chance."

I shook off a feeling of doom and tried to smile brightly for the public.

Rory piled out of the weighing room with the other jockeys, heading straight for the centre of the ring where I'd turned in Murphy. The parade ring was jostling with proud owners, some so new to the game that they struggled to recognize their own horses.

The Guv'nor hissed instructions to Rory

without moving his lips but they carried on the breeze and made my blood run cold.

"You can't keep him boxed in!" I yelped, swivelling my head round to a tight-lipped Rory. "He's a front runner, if he gets jostled he'll panic."

By now I was holding up the queue of horses but I didn't care. "You've got to let him have his head."

Murphy was already dark with sweat and half rearing at the entrance to the course.

"I take orders from the Guv'nor." Rory kicked Murphy forward. "Now unclip the ruddy thing before I get fined for obstruction."

I couldn't watch the race. I hid behind the saddling stalls, a jittering wreck. "Please, let him be safe. Please, just let him get round in one piece."

Everyone was converging on the grandstand. The commentary rolled on, charting the action. "And they're coming to the third, heading out into the back straight . . . It's Peeper's Bay behind Lucky Robin followed closely by Murphy's Law . . ."

I couldn't bear it. I ran down towards a clutch of people gathered at the last fence. I could see a blur of horses rounding a bend. The commentator faltered, alarm bristling. Something was happening. The horses were bunching tight. There was a gasp from the people with binoculars.

"What's happening?" I croaked.

The commentator answered my question. Murphy's Law had crashed in panic through the white barrier and was dragging Rory behind him.

Eight

I let out a strangled sob. My voice seemed to be wedged in my throat, somewhere along with my heart. All I could see was my beloved horse gripped in mindless panic. And Rory. Oh poor Rory.

I ran until my lungs felt as if they were bleeding. The grandstand had gone deathly quiet. Mr Chips suddenly appeared, thundering behind Murphy with a head collar and a feed bucket. Murphy slowed down.

"Oh thank God." Rory's foot came out of the stirrup but he lay crumpled and lifeless on the ground. The paramedics swarmed in, blocking him from view as the ambulance came closer.

"Murphy!" The big, chestnut horse threw up his head, recognizing my voice.

The hurdle race was still in progress, mechanically turning into the home straight, but nobody was interested.

"Whoa, boy, steady now." He trotted towards

me, snorting with relief. I held on to his mane while I threaded the reins out from his legs. Miraculously, he was unhurt, his sides just heaved.

"Take him back to Gertie." I stuffed the reins in Mr Chips's hands. Murphy was snatching for air like a deep-sea diver. I hurtled towards the ambulance. They were loading Rory in on a stretcher. The Guv'nor was already there with a steward.

"Rory!" Tears sprang out of my eyes.

The Guv'nor clamped a steadying hand on my shoulder, pushing me back.

"Calm down, Justina, he's just badly concussed. He's broken his leg but nothing else. He's going to be all right."

When we got to the hospital he'd been rushed in for an emergency operation. We drank lukewarm coffee and sat on plastic chairs, waiting for news for what seemed like hours.

The Guv'nor talked of jockeys' injuries as if they were colds and flu. "Internal injuries, split livers and punctured lungs are horrible, but head and back injuries are the worst." He made it sound as if Rory had got off with toothache. His last stable jockey had broken his right collar bone eleven times and his left four times, not to mention practically every other bone in his body. I fingered my polystyrene cup and prayed it would never happen to me.

"I'd better report to Badger so he can inform

the lads." The Guv'nor went towards the public phone. "The only one who'll be pleased about this is Jacko. He'll be taking over all the rides."

I spilt my coffee all over my lap.

That evening I lovingly tended Murphy's legs, coating on gel and carefully bandaging them to reduce any filling. As quickly as I finished, Gertie was wickedly pulling them off. I outfoxed her by rooting out Chelsea's muzzle, kept specially for his trips to the vet, and fixing it on her.

It wasn't long before Jacko poked his head over the door, hardly able to contain his excitement. It made me feel sick. He'd gelled back his black hair and dug out a leather jacket for a night on the town. He grinned at me wolfishly and rubbed the stubble on his chin. "What that 'orse needs is a good thrashing, teach it some manners." His eyes hardened to pebbles. "And I'm just the jock to do it."

I went as rigid as an ironing board and mentally vowed to break every whip on the premises.

Straight after first lot the next morning, I caught the bus into Cheltenham to visit Rory. A plan was forming in my head as I clutched the letter that had just arrived from the Jockey Club and fingered the date for my jockey's licence.

I paced up the endless hospital passages, feeling more nauseous by the minute. Rory had been moved to his own room because the women from the ward next door had kept on trying to ambush him. It wasn't my imagination that all the nurses looked dewy-eyed and made endless excuses to visit room 6A.

My heart wobbled when I saw him propped up in bed, reading *Horse and Hound*. His right leg was in plaster now, right up his thigh, and he had a knitting needle ready to thwart any itches. He looked grumpy and bored out of his brain.

"That dunce of a horse of yours—"

"Don't call Murphy names," I barked. "I told you not to hold him up."

He scowled and threw the magazine across the bed. "You realize I'll lose the Championship because of this."

"You can win it back next year."

He didn't say anything.

I perched on the bed, scrunching a couple of empty sweet wrappers and tried not to let him see my hands shaking. "There's something I want to ask you."

His gorgeous eyes narrowed until the long lashes nearly touched. I looked away quickly and wiped my hands on my jeans. "I want you to teach me to be a jockey."

"Are you crazy?"

I crashed on and showed him the letter.

"Why do you girls always have a romantic notion of racing?" he groaned.

"You know I'm good," I leapt up defensively. "And besides, it'll keep you occupied. What else would you be doing in here, apart from rotting your teeth and reading Dick Francis? I could keep you informed on Dolphin Barn, tell you what Jacko's up to."

"Wacko Jacko," Rory grunted, "the man who's in love with his own ego."

"Exactly. If I start getting rides, it'll rattle his cage."

Rory looked thoughtful.

"I could look after Poppy for you, dust your flat, water the plants."

A tinge of colour started creeping into his waxy white cheeks. He didn't speak for a few moments then, "Have you any idea what nerves of steel you have to have to be a jockey?" he asked. "When you're coming into a fence and you know your horse isn't going to jump. You know you're a faller and twenty or so horses are going to come over you in a stampede?" He stared straight at me, eyeball to eyeball.

"But that's the downside. Things go wrong all the time, every day, but every so often they go wonderfully, gloriously right. That's what we do it for." I shut up and gnawed my lip, silently pleading.

He burst into a full-on grin which lit up his face. "You're the pluckiest lass I've ever met. Here." He pulled a set of keys from the bedside table. "Pick up Poppy from my neighbour, don't water the cactus. Get a bin liner from under the sink and bring back every video you can lay your hands on that isn't *Fantasy Football* or *Wallace and Grommit*."

I flung my arms round his neck and kissed him on a prickly cheek. Then I snatched back and wondered what on earth I'd done. But he wasn't looking horrified, so I dredged up some composure and flew out into the corridor, just missing a meal trolley full of dishes of semolina.

With Rory out of the way, Jacko was even more of a bore than anyone had anticipated. Within days, the lads whose horses Jacko had raced were moaning that the animals had been pushed too hard. There was a queue of people with complaints outside the Guv'nor's door every morning. But, to add insult to injury, Jacko was getting results and the Guv'nor turned a convenient deaf ear.

Before the end of the week, Harris had resigned and Scottie was sporting a white shirt with the words "Come Back, Rory. All is Forgiven". Mandy was walking around like a panda with permanently streaked mascara because Jacko kept calling her "pork chops" in front of owners. Stable morale was at an all-time low when Jacko wormed his way on to the front page of the local paper claiming that he was going to be the new conditional champion jockey. Even Shona was feeling the rough edge of his tongue.

"You've got to do something," I moaned to Rory in my afternoon breaks, clocking the increasing number of personalized messages on his cast. "He's a tyrant, a bully, an egomaniac and he's breaking the horses."

The previous night in bed I'd bawled my eyes out just thinking about Jacko riding my precious Murphy. He'd taken to standing outside the stable during grooming, and cracking his knuckles, exuding meanness. Gertie had boiled over and rammed his knees with bone-clashing accuracy. I knew she'd die for Murphy but it wouldn't be long before the Guv'nor put him back on a race-course.

Rory had thrown himself wholeheartedly into teaching me every jockey's trick in the book. Watching races over and over stopped him sinking into an abyss of depression. It lifted his spirits, sparked hope.

The whole hospital now knew he was a patient and he had more roses than the Chelsea Flower Show. He'd pleaded with a female doctor to keep him in a few more days because his mother was hovering in the wings ready to cook him enormous meals which would blow up his weight. He was gradually mastering the art of crutches and spent every morning in the children's ward bringing magic laughter to sick little faces. He was so gorgeous! Now I had to psych myself up outside his door every day so as not to give my feelings for him away. He must never know how I really felt. I hadn't forgotten him and Shona. I wasn't going to be just another girl in his line of conquests.

One evening when I went to see him, Rory was propped up in bed reading *Hello* magazine, which fell open at pictures of Frankie Dettori with his new son.

"Best ambassador racing's seen since Jenny Pitman," he grinned.

"But so much better looking," I drooled, flicking over the pages. A cloud crossed Rory's face, but he didn't say anything.

The nurses had been incredible in rustling up a video machine from a disused day room. I'd watched so many races I felt like a commentator. The only thing Rory hadn't been able to wangle was Sky Racing Channel.

I had some brilliant news but before I could tell him, Rory asked, as usual, if I'd been sticking to my training schedule.

Jump jockeys have to be unbelievably fit and Rory said at the moment I'd be dead after half a circuit. From the luxury of watching soaps at night curled up with Smokey I was dragging myself to Cheltenham swimming baths and clocking up seventy lengths, then wilting in Rory's room doing sit-ups, press-ups, and tying myself in knots with a skipping rope. I was beyond exhaustion and I was as lean as a greyhound.

"You can't afford to dawdle." Rory pressed play and we started to watch yet another race on the video. "If there's a Martin Pipe horse in the race it will usually set the pace. Don't get left behind. Speaking of which," he fast-forwarded to a rare mistake by Richard Dunwoody, "let the reins travel through your fingers. Don't hinder the horse. Keep your weight back. It's the only way you'll stay on board."

I pored over each race with fierce concentration. "Don't expect favours from the other riders, they'll be out to cut you up. If someone starts shouting, ignore them, it'll be another case of trying to intimidate you. Female jocks are about as popular as terrorists. Don't forget it."

I felt as if a shoal of anxious fishes were quivering in my stomach.

"Don't let your brain turn to porridge. Keep your wits about you. Be ready to change plan. Races rarely unfold how you expect them. And hold your nerve. The best jocks have complete control of themselves."

I clutched my stomach as if I'd gone over a hump-backed bridge at ninety miles an hour. The dream I'd cherished all my life was starting to take shape.

"And congratulations." Rory snapped off the video and looked right in my eyes.

"How did you know?" I gasped.

"Because I figured you didn't win the lottery, and if you grin any wider you'll split your head open."

I poured out my story then. How I'd been offered a last-minute cancellation at Cheltenham racecourse and I was now a fully fledged apprentice jockey. I could ride in races, with certain restrictions. I was a step nearer to partnering Murphy. And to taking on the greats.

I hugged Rory awkwardly. The future was about living on the edge, sacrifice and single-mindedness. Most people experience highs and lows, elation and despair occasionally, but for a jump jockey it is the daily agenda. I crossed my fingers and knew Murphy would keep me safe.

"I'll see you tomorrow." Rory flicked the television to *Coronation Street* and became immediately engrossed. I knew he wanted to be alone. It was chewing him up that he couldn't ride. It showed in the colour of his skin, the slump of his shoulders, the haunted emptiness in his brown eyes. But nothing could take away my own soaring happiness. I'd turned a corner, was climbing the hill.

The stables were in darkness. A silver sheen on the tarmac suggested a frost in the morning. Like a galoot I clattered straight into the bin, which hadn't been emptied for weeks, and stubbed my toe. Poppy started barking and bounding up at the kitchen window. Within seconds the fluorescent light blinked on and Mandy appeared, white-faced and swollen-eyed, at the door.

"Thank God you're back," she breathed. "Something dreadful's happened."

Nine

Leonora was curled up at the back of the stable, trembling convulsively. Sweat poured off her, staining her coat. As I approached, she rolled her eyes and flinched as if she didn't trust a soul in the world.

"Leonora." You wouldn't take her for the same horse. "What happened?" I croaked, parched by the pain of it. "As if I can't guess."

Mandy shuddered, clutching her dressing-gown round her Peter Rabbit nightshirt. "Jacko. He lost his temper on the run in. Went for it hammer and tongs with his whip. The good news is he's been suspended for twenty-one days and the Guv'nor's sacked him. He was suppposed to give her an easy ride."

For a moment my breath swamped my chest. It was as if my heart had no room to beat. Poor Leonora, she didn't deserve this. I stroked her and cooed to her over and over like a mother protecting her child.

"He's a pig," Mandy muttered, eyes welling with tears. "I hate him."

"Where is he now?" I wanted to commit murder.

"Skulked off with some mates to the pub. Some of the lads have been looking for him, wanted to teach him a lesson. She won, you know, ran her heart out . . . she gave everything." Mandy broke off, wiping her eyes on her sleeve.

I went into the tack room at first light to make a cup of coffee. Badger was already starting with the feed trolley down the other side of the yard. I heard a noise from the corner by the rug chests and nearly leapt out of my skin. Jacko was tied up and gagged, stripped to his boxer shorts with a concoction of what looked like hoof oil, marmalade and raw egg rubbed into his hair. I could see the gooseflesh on his bare arms and legs and the fury in his eyes. He'd been well and truly done over and I wasn't going to breathe a word to the Guv'nor. Quietly, I closed the door and left Poppy enthusiastically licking egg yolk off the end of his nose.

"He said no, didn't he?" I clutched the sink unit, feeling sick and light-headed.

Rory clacked his crutches awkwardly in an attempt to sit down next to Smokey. I didn't look at the washed-out face, the dark ringed eyes. I spun round and stared instead at the pile of mouldering pots, not knowing how I was going to function now.

"I know what this is about, he doesn't want to lose a stablehand, doesn't want the rest of the staff getting ideas. He's so selfish he won't even think about giving me a chance." I gulped back tears and picked neurotically at my nails.

Rory shifted uncomfortably. It was a week since Jacko had been sacked and up to now the Guv'nor had been booking freelance jockeys through an agent.

"He called me Robert a lot and talked about house insurance," Rory ventured.

Typical. He couldn't even give a straight answer. Smokey shot out of the cat flap preferring the cold to the tension inside.

"He said to give you these." Rory passed over a crumpled Tesco carrier bag. Probably some socks the Guv wanted darning and thought it was suitable women's work. Bitterness rose in my throat like bile.

I tore into the bag and the Dolphin Barn silks slid to the floor. For a second I blinked helplessly and the black and burgundy colours blurred into the lino. Then I picked them up, holding them to the light with reverence.

"Murphy's entered for a three-mile chase at Warwick in ten days' time. The Guv'nor said he's putting you up."

Rory waited for the explosion but it didn't

come. It was so unexpected I was numb to elation. My brain was so shocked it couldn't relay the right signals. In the end, I just burst into tears and dripped salt water all over the precious Dolphin Barn colours.

"What do you think?" I stood trembling in front of the mirror, smoothing the parachute-like silk over my hips, revelling in the feel and the look.

Mandy tried to talk with her mouth full of pins. Luckily, it wasn't too big by much. Hurriedly, with rubber hands, I pulled on breeches and boots for the complete look. On the day I'd wear a thin Lycra polo neck under the colours and 40 denier tights. And a back protector. I was shaking like a reed.

Mandy flushed with satisfaction as she made the last tuck. "You look like a model."

"Oh, blast!" I was horrified. "You're right, I look as if I've just stepped out of a catalogue." Without stopping for a second I grabbed Mandy's scissors and slashed off a clump of hair, starting by my left ear.

"What are you doing?"

By the time Mandy was galvanized into action, I'd hacked off every tress of my long brown hair and was standing with a carpet of it at my feet. I was giddy with the thrill.

"There." I patted the pudding-bowl style. "Now I look like a proper jockey."

"You're crackers, do you know that?" Mandy gasped, her face drained of blood. "Is there nothing you'll not do to win a race?"

Murphy was in top form, revelling in all the attention and nodding his head at passers-by in his own version of the royal wave. Everyone wanted Murphy to do well. There were horses in the yard entering group one races with famous jockeys on board, but all anyone could talk about was the novice chase at Warwick and our very own Bumper Velvet. It was as if we'd caught the imagination of the whole yard. Even Badger was full of advice and kept an eagle eye on Murphy, as if he were set in gold plate.

Rory kept up a strict exercise programme and I stepped up to riding out four horses a day. The top jockeys have so many race rides they keep unbelievably fit, which gives them an advantage over the less well-known. I had to drink two pints of full cream milk a day and give up chocolate and crisps. I couldn't sleep at night and I could barely eat. My nerves were stretched to breaking point.

Two days before the race we crowded into the Guv'nor's office to watch tapes from Warwick and past races of the other horses competing. There was Rory, Badger, Mandy, Scooby, Mr Chips and Scottie and Roy Rogers, not to mention Chelsea and Poppy who seemed to have become firm friends.

The main challenge was going to come from a rangy brown horse called Heritage Bay who was an established front runner and likely to take on Murphy. After watching two videos of his races at Warwick, we all noticed, to much hooting and jeering from Scottie and Roy Rogers, that he always ran wide off the bottom bend.

"Sit tight if he's making the pace and, when he runs wide, nip up the inside." The Guv'nor barked out orders while wrestling with a jar of pickled onions. A cushion fight between Mandy and Scooby got out of control and Rory yelped as a flying missile hit his leg. Poppy tried to plonk her bottom on my knee and accidentally slid off.

One thing we'd learnt about Murphy was that he always had a flat spot in the middle of his work rides. He'd be off the bridle, not responding to his rider, for half a furlong and if you didn't know him you'd think he'd run out of petrol, but then turbo power would kick in and he'd be off again like a rocket.

Our tactics were to get far enough ahead before that happened so nobody could tail us. We watched three more horses but didn't think they'd be serious contenders. Warwick was a track made for galloping, with a golf course in the middle. It tended to favour good jumpers but trainers didn't usually send them to Warwick. We'd quickly found out that Murphy would plough through anything small or flimsy in disgust. He needed good solid fences.

"He'll walk it." Badger had every confidence. Nobody referred to the disastrous first-time effort which had left Rory with a shattered leg.

Even Shona managed to swallow her jealousy and pop in for part of the action. I couldn't quite believe that these same people, only a few months ago, had put maggots on my chair and superglued my boots to the tack room floor. Now they were rooting for me like family. In racing, the endless practical jokes are all part and parcel of the sport. It has something to do with the reckless lifestyle of riding racehorses.

I was glad I was in the thick of it. It was in my bones, my blood, my heart. And in forty-eight hours I'd be under starter's orders.

"Get him away early and take it wide." The Guv'nor prodded the ground of Warwick racecourse with a walking stick and blew through his lips. "The grass is too long."

I tried to wrench my thoughts into order. At 3.20 I'd have to give the performance of my life and already my brain felt like sodden sponge. I jogged haplessly after the Guv'nor, recoiling from the solid black fences which seemed to loom larger from the ground the more you looked at them. I was shaking until my teeth chattered. A biting wind ripped straight through us, but the Guv'nor didn't seem to notice. Racecourses have a lot in common with seaside piers.

"Justina, for heaven's sake, pay attention." The Guv'nor was treading in a clod of turf in front of an open ditch running downhill. "Now, the fences will come up quick in the back straight. You've got to be ready for them. But don't override. If you go on a long stride, you'll tip up. Sit tight and don't interfere."

My arms and legs wilted. I could barely talk, let alone walk. Nerves had clamped my whole body.

Back at the horsebox the Guv'nor passed me the tiny racing saddle. Then he frogmarched me to the weighing room where all the jockeys got changed and pushed me into a cubicle off the main building. "If you need any help, ask Rory's valet."

I breathed in the smell of must and cobwebs. Undiluted terror was ripping through me. I somehow fumbled on my silks but couldn't tie the cap over my jockey skull. I groaned, almost like a howl. 3.03. Seventeen minutes. I made a split-second decision and grabbed my gloves and goggles.

The waft of men's aftershave in the main room nearly knocked me out. A portable telly blared out from the food table. It was giving the odds – Murphy was 50–1. A ginger-haired jockey pushed past wearing nothing but tights. I spotted the valet, Jim Ealey and, eyes stinging with cigarette smoke, somehow staggered across to him.

He was helping a jockey with dark hair who I instantly recognized as the last winner of the Grand National. He had his head in his hands, focusing on the race ahead and ignoring the jokes and mickey-taking from the other lads. I crumpled on to the bench, shaking and praying the valet would notice me.

I was mad to think I could take on professional jockeys. They looked so tough, a steamroller wouldn't flatten them. I'd made a mistake. Better to withdraw now than let everyone down. Jacko was right, I wasn't cut out for this. Maybe the Guv'nor would give me my old job back – I'd happily scrub out the mash barrow for the next ten years.

"Miss Brooks." The valet beamed down at me. "Now, let's have a look at your helmet, shall we?"

I weighed in and carried my saddle out to the Guv'nor in a complete blur. All I was aware of was that it was raining in blinding sheets. We had to go back into the weighing room for the last few minutes. Everyone was moaning about the weather. Nobody spoke to me. I was like a fly on the wall, insignificant. I was beyond nerves now, just a numb heap waiting for the inevitable.

The clock over the door reached eleven minutes past three. You could smell the tension and anticipation, like stale sweat. Everybody was psyching up for the task ahead.

An official walked in, gloomy with wet. "Jockeys, please."

Ten

For one panicked moment I couldn't spot the Guv'nor or Murphy in the parade ring. My shoulders sagged and my head dropped like a stone. Any afternoon light had been blotted out by the pewter grey clouds. A thin string of punters gathered near the corner where Heritage Bay had turned in, hot favourite at 5–1. And then Murphy's familar neigh rattled out round the stands as he burst from behind some cherry trees, towing Scooby who was doing all he could to hold him. He towered above the other horses and bulldozed across the manicured green grass, thumping his nose into my stomach for Polo mints. I started to feel human again – hope coursed into my veins.

The Guv'nor and Rory battled through the rain, carrying rugs and binoculars. Seeing Rory was another boost. He'd made a special effort to support me. He was in my corner, and people were noticing.

"He's got some ginger in him," Scooby whispered as Murphy stamped and fidgeted and threw his head sky-high so I couldn't straighten the burgundy-and-black velvet browband which I'd bought specially to match my colours. It was an old racing term. Scooby meant he was full of beans.

"All the lads have put a tenner a piece on him, straight on the nose," he whispered and then nearly got trodden on as Murphy barged forward, hardly able to contain his excitement.

"Give it your best shot." The Guv'nor examined his fingernails ferociously, raindrops plinking off his trilby which looked as if it had been chewed at by mice. "But come back safe," he muttered, dark hooded eyes confirming his anxiety.

Jockeys were mounting. A fresh sheet of rain drove sideways into my face. I wanted Rory to say something, touch my shoulder, hold my eyes, anything, but he just stared into space, hard lines of tension pencilled down each side of his mouth. It couldn't have been easy, watching his colleagues out there doing what he loved most.

"Three, two, one!" Scooby gave me a leg up into the saddle. I gathered the reins and fumbled for the stirrups. The miniscule saddle was as slippery as an eel. Murphy threw up his neck and plunged forward. There was no time for nerves now, self-preservation took over.

The Guv'nor shouted something but it was whipped away in the wind. He was left rooted to the grass in the parade ring, gaunt and wired with tension, the race completely out of his hands.

I sucked in the wet air and felt Murphy's power erupt in a volley of bucks. He wanted to race, he was thriving on every second, plunging to get out there.

"Watch it!" The jockey behind nearly had his horse's teeth kicked out.

Scooby unclipped the lead rope. There was no extra time. The last thing I saw was his rain-soaked face as we burst on to the racecourse turf in a sea of horses. It was just the two of us now – against nineteen other horses and twenty-two fences.

I mustn't fall off before the start. I mustn't. I mustn't. Horses filed down the inside, spraying mud into my face. I held Murphy together, containing his massive energy on what felt like reins of cotton thread. By the time we stopped at the first fence, my calves were shaking. The grandstand and hordes of people seemed a million miles away. The quietness was unnerving.

The ginger-haired jockey I'd seen in the weighing room pulled up alongside and practically rammed my knee. "Keep your brute out of my way," he muttered. "Or else. I don't want a girl stuffing up my chances." His jaw hardly moved so I couldn't even feel sure he'd said anything at all. But one thought was thumping between my temples. I had to get away early – or they'd cut me up. And it wouldn't be accidental.

We turned back from the black birch fence and circled, ready for the starter. Murphy fretted and trembled, and rain mixed with sweat to produce a frothy foam on his neck. I hauled him across to the outside, creating a yawning gap from the other horses bunched on the rail, but we were clear of trouble.

I circled three times. Jockeys hedged back and forth. Horses snorted. The starting tape jagged up. We were off.

I lost my breath in the first few strides as Murphy threw himself into the bridle and whip-lashed my neck. He hurled at the first fence with wild abandon and seemed to be in the air for hours. I lost all reason, my brain mulched as pure speed took over.

Halfway round the track and the ground sucked and popped as hooves went in. But Murphy skipped along, eating it. And every other horse laboured in his wake, long lengths behind.

He wasted energy in flamboyant displays of jumping, which weren't lost on the crowds. As we streaked past the grandstand a great roar rose out of the rain and Murphy grew two inches. He was so pleased with himself, he turned to gawp at the people and nearly missed his stride at the water. I had to kick him in the ribs to get his mind back on the job.

It was miraculous, incredible, the buzz I'd craved all my life. I was sitting on a jumping machine, a power engine to which nobody had given the time of day. He was my glory.

As we turned into the racecourse for the second time, the rain found a new vengeance. It came down in blinding sweeps and Murphy ducked his head between his knees and fought on like a tank. We still had a long way to go.

The sinews in my legs were starting to twang now like violin strings. I couldn't see a thing. Murphy started jumping to the left and made a clouting mistake at one of the easiest fences on the course. It was heavier going second time round and I could feel him straining to lift his shoulders.

Pounding hooves drummed behind but I couldn't see how close they were. I concentrated on helping Murphy, coaxing him, urging him not to lose heart. Four fences from home and his petrol gauge dipped. I felt him slow up, coast, lose valuable seconds. There was nothing I could do. Just sit tight. I kept him on a short stride, carried him over the next fence.

Suddenly the race seemed to click into slow motion. Heritage Bay loomed upsides, getting up, staying on, jumping like a stag. He overtook Murphy, a blur of yellow silk shooting past. Mud kicked up, filling my mouth. We couldn't be beaten. We couldn't . . .

I felt Murphy deaden, dispirited. But then his ears flashed back and he tore forward, digging into his energy reserves, running on guts and courage. "Come on, Murphy, come on, my brave, brave horse!" I rode him out arms and legs, together as one, exhausted but game.

The wind and rain changed direction as we thundered towards the bottom bend. It was behind us, on our side, buffeting us on. Murphy made a huge leap at the last, standing off outside the wings. I gasped in shock. Only he could pull it off. He landed perfectly and snatched back valuable lengths. Then he lowered his head and started to run.

A great roar went up from the crowds. Blinking, unbelieving, I saw the gap open up as Heritage Bay drifted wide. We had our chance . . .

I visualized the Governor watching, tense, irate, yelling instructions. The commentary became crystal clear. "*Murphy's Law is finishing strongly, he's making ground on Heritage Bay. Murphy's Law is getting up . . . Murphy's Law is getting up! It's Justina Brooks. It's number eight . . .*"

A wall of sound burst from the grandstand. People leapt up cheering. Murphy responded. Wafting his big ears he snaked his head down in one last gallant effort. Both horses flashed past the winning post, neck and neck. Both had given their all. But Murphy had given a piece of his heart and soul.

I collapsed on his neck. I could hear myself making crying noises but the tears refused to come. I was in shock.

"Don't look so upset. You've won!" The jockey on Heritage Bay rode across and pumped my hand but it still didn't register. And then Scooby was running forward and behind him the Guv'nor. And Scottie. And Badger. And they were all grinning, and crying, and acting like goons.

It could have been the Gold Cup. All around, people streamed forward, wanting to touch the chestnut horse, the rain and the gloom forgotten. It occurred to me then that Murphy was more than just a racehorse. He touched people's hearts. They could relate to his almost human qualities. He was going to be a celebrity. And everybody today had seen that specialness.

It was announced on the public address system as we battled through to the winner's enclosure: *"First: Number eight. Murphy's Law. Ridden by Miss Justina Brooks. Owned and trained by Mr Kenneth Brown."*

I slid off, feeling the ground come up to meet me. Hands reached out, grasping at my silks. I had to get the saddle off, but there was no strength left in my arms. Murphy stood proud, his chest and legs splattered with thick, black mud. Cameras clicked and flashed. A TV reporter pushed forward, and as the crowd parted I saw my parents, smiling proudly and waving at me.

"Go and weigh in," the Guv'nor growled, bringing a sense of reality to things. I'd been examining Murphy's legs. Where was Rory?

Somehow I groped back to the weighing room and followed procedure. I had to get back to Murphy, though, to check he was all right. But, instead, I crumpled on to the bench under the coats and tried to come to terms with the churning emotions in my head. I'd won. My first race. All those years of dreaming. Wanting. Believing. Riding a broom stick round the garden pretending it was Red Rum. Rigging up a saddle on the back of the sofa.

I buried my face in someone's duffle coat and felt a blob of dried mud crumble off my face. I had to get changed. Clean myself up. But the tears of relief and amazement poured out in a never-ending flow.

"Justina?" Someone brushed back the coats and stuffed a huge white hanky under my nose. I still couldn't see anything apart from a tartan lining and a black scarf, but the voice was unmistakable.

"Rory?"

"I never want to go through that again," he groaned.

I stopped sniffling in mid-stream and felt my heart flip over and disappear into my stomach.

"All the time in the paddock, I couldn't even

look at you, I was so nervous. I was rigid with worry."

Something in his voice sent an electric shock zooming up my spine. What was he trying to say?

I sneaked a look under the coat's arm and was lost in gorgeous dark hair and eyes fiercely concentrating on the muddy floor.

"Justina, there's something I've got to tell you."

I jumped a foot in the air. Then he ripped back my protective screen and leant close, inches from my face. His eyes burnt into mine and I melted under the intensity of his gaze.

I couldn't cope with this. I wouldn't be able to pretend. My heart hammered and I could feel my face betraying how I felt. But I couldn't look down either because his right hand was now cupping my jaw and he was drinking in my face, – and his lips were moving closer . . .

"Justina, where the dickens are you?" The Guv'nor crashed into the weighing room hotly pursued by Scooby and Scottie, shattering the moment into a thousand pieces.

"Channel Four want an interview," the Guv'nor roared, practically shooing me out with his umbrella. "And there's the prizegiving."

"I can't!" My throat came unstuck at the thought of talking on telly.

"If I can do it, so can you," he barked. "You're in the public eye now good and proper, got to give 'em what they want."

As I stepped out into the winner's enclosure once again and the huge champion's plaque glinted in the watery sun, I knew my life had changed for ever. I was up with the professionals now, every step and move monitored. But as reporters and microphones crammed round, eager to relive the race, my heart strayed back to the weighing room and that lost, treasured moment. I'd made it as a jockey, but would Rory Calligan ever become my boyfriend?

Glossary

box walker – A horse which paces round its stable endlessly, fretting and wearing itself out.

chaps – Usually made of leather, they are worn over trousers as protection against dirt while riding.

filling – Swelling.

First/second lot – The first and second work rides of the day.

furlong – An eighth of a mile.

guinea – The equivalent of £1.05.

seller – Also called a claims race, where the horses can be bought for a set price after s/he has run.

steeplechase – A horse race with a set number of obstacles including a water jump. Originally a cross-country race from town steeple to town steeple.

surcingle – A belt or strap used to keep a day or night rug in position.

upsides – Riding alongside another horse.

Winners 2
Crossing the Line

Justina Brooks knows that with Murphy's Law she will one day win the Grand National, but in the tough world of racing not everyone agrees. After all, Murphy is a difficult horse and no girl has done it before. When the people at her stables, Dolphin Barn, seem to lose faith in her, Justina decides to prove them all wrong. She races at Ascot, for rich, rival trainer, Adam Valentine.

But pride often comes before a fall. Will racing for Valentine be the start of a more glamorous career, or the beginning of the end of her dreams?

Jump into the second book in the exciting Winners series!

If you enjoyed *Winners*, you'll love . . .

Hollywell Stables
Samantha Alexander

Hollywell Stables – sanctuary for horses and ponies – and a dream come true for Mel, Ross and Katie . . .

Join the gang on their adventures in this fantastic eight-book series.

Praise for *Hollywell Stables*:

'*Hollywell Stables* is the vanguard of the new breed of pony stories . . . these are cracking stories.' *TES*

'The action comes thick and fast with adventure after adventure rolling off each page.' *Riding Magazine*

A selected list of SAMANTHA ALEXANDER books available from Macmillan

The prices shown below are correct at the time of going to press. However, Macmillan Publishers reserve the right to show new retail prices on covers which may differ from those previously advertised.

WINNERS

1. Racing Start	0 330	48438 9	£3.99
2. Crossing the Line	0 330	48439 7	£3.99

HOLLYWELL STABLES

1. Flying Start	0 330	33639 8	£2.99
2. The Gamble	0 330	33685 1	£2.99
3. The Chase	0 330	33857 9	£2.99
4. Fame	0 330	33858 7	£2.99
5. The Mission	0 330	34199 5	£2.99
6. Trapped	0 330	34200 2	£2.99
7. Running Wild	0 330	34201 0	£2.99
8. Secrets	0 330	34202 9	£2.99

All Macmillan titles can be ordered at your local bookshop or are available by post from:

Book Service by Post
PO Box 29, Douglas, Isle of Man IM99 1BQ

Credit cards accepted. For details:
Telephone: 01624 675137
Fax: 01624 670923
E-mail: bookshop@enterprise.net

Free postage and packing in the UK.
Overseas customers: add £1 per book (paperback)
and £3 per book (hardback).